# NIGHT AND DAY

ALSO BY ROBERT
B. PARKER

**Resolution**
**Appaloosa**
**Double Play**
**Gunman's Rhapsody**
**All Our Yesterdays**
**A Year at the Races**
  (with Joan H. Parker)

**Perchance to Dream**
**Poodle Springs**
  (with Raymond
  Chandler)
**Love and Glory**
**Wilderness**
**Three Weeks in Spring**
  (with Joan H. Parker)
**Training with Weights**
  (with John R. Marsh)

# NIGHT AND DAY

ROBERT B. PARKER

**Doubleday Large Print
Home Library Edition**

G. P. Putnam's Sons

*New York*

This Large Print Edition, prepared especially for Double-day Large Print Home Library, contains the complete, unabridged text of the original Publisher's Edition.

PUTNAM

G. P. PUTNAM'S SONS
**Publishers Since 1838**
Published by the Penguin Group
Penguin Group (USA) Inc., 375 Hudson Street, New York, New York 10014, USA • Penguin Group (Canada), 90 Eglinton Avenue East, Suite 700, Toronto, Ontario M4P 2Y3, Canada (a division of Pearson Canada Inc.) • Penguin Books Ltd, 80 Strand, London WC2R 0RL, England • Penguin Ireland, 25 St Stephen's Green, Dublin 2, Ireland (a division of Penguin Books Ltd) • Penguin Group (Australia), 250 Camberwell Road, Camberwell, Victoria 3124, Australia (a division of Pearson Australia Group Pty Ltd) • Penguin Books India Pvt Ltd, 11 Community Centre, Panchsheel Park, New Delhi– 110 017, India • Penguin Group (NZ), 67 Apollo Drive, Rosedale, North Shore 0632, New Zealand (a division of Pearson New Zealand Ltd) • Penguin Books (South Africa) (Pty) Ltd, 24 Sturdee Avenue, Rosebank, Johannesburg 2196, South Africa

Penguin Books Ltd, Registered Offices: 80 Strand, London WC2R 0RL, England

**This Large Print Book carries the
Seal of Approval of N.A.V.H.**

**For Joan:**
**Only you beneath the moon**
**and under the sun.**

# NIGHT AND DAY

# 1

Jesse Stone sat in his office at the Paradise police station, looking at the sign painted on the pebbled-glass window of his office door. From the inside it read *FEIHC*, or it would have, if the letters hadn't been backward. He tried pronouncing the word, decided he couldn't, and stopped thinking about it. On his desk was a glamour head shot of his ex-wife. He looked at it for a time, and decided not to think about that, either.

Molly Crane came from the front desk and opened the door.

"Suit just called in," she said. "There's

some kind of disturbance at the junior high school and he thinks you and I ought to come down."

"Girls involved?" Jesse said.

"That's why he wants me," Molly said.

"I understand," Jesse said. "But why does he want me?"

"You're the chief of police," Molly said. "Everybody wants you."

Jesse glanced at Jenn's picture again.

"Oh," Jesse said. "Yeah."

Jesse stood, and clipped his gun to his belt.

"Though you sure don't dress like a chief," Molly said.

Jesse was wearing a uniform shirt, blue jeans, Nikes, a dark blue Paradise police baseball hat, and a badge that said *Chief.* He tapped the badge.

"I do where it counts," he said. "Who's on the desk?"

"Steve," Molly said.

"Okay," Jesse said. "You drive. No siren."

"Oh, damn," Molly said. "I never get to use the siren."

"Maybe when you make sergeant," Jesse said.

There were two Paradise police cruisers parked outside of the junior high school.

"Who's in the other cruiser," Jesse said as they got out of the car.

"Eddie Cox," Molly said. "He and Suit have seven to eleven this week."

They walked into the school lobby, where a thick mill of parents was being held at bay by two Paradise cops. Most of the parents were mothers, with a scatter of fathers looking oddly out of place. When Jesse came in they all swarmed toward him, many of them speaking to him loudly.

"You're the chief of police, are you gonna do something?"

"I want that woman arrested!"

"She's a goddamned child molester!"

"What are you going to do about this?"

"Do you know what she did?"

"Did they tell you what happened here?"

Jesse ignored them.

He said to Molly, "Keep them here."

Then he pointed at Suit and jerked his head down the hallway.

"What's up," Jesse said when they were alone.

Simpson's real name was Luther. He was a big kid, with blond hair and a round face. He wasn't as young as he looked, but he was young. He was called Suitcase after the baseball player, Harry "Suitcase" Simpson.

"This is weird," Suit said.

Jesse waited.

"Mrs. Ingersoll," Suit said, "the principal. Christ, she was principal when I was here."

Jesse waited.

"There was some kind of after-school dance yesterday," Suit said, his voice speeding up a little. "Eighth-grade dance. And before the dance, Mrs. Ingersoll took all the girls into the girls' locker room and picked up their dresses to see what kind of underwear they had on."

Jesse stared at Suit for a time without speaking.

Then Jesse said, "Huh?"

"That's what the girls claim."

"Why did she do that?" Jesse said.

"Don't know," Suit said. "But when the girls got home a lot of them told their mothers, and . . ." He gestured toward the crowd.

Jesse nodded.

"Where's Mrs. Ingersoll?" Jesse said.

"In her office."

"You ask her about this?" Jesse said.

"She called in and said there was a disturbance. So we came down here and found what you see. It was like a damned lynch mob. We sort of wrangled them into the lobby, and Mrs. Ingersoll went in her office and won't come out, which is when we called you . . . and"—Suitcase looked a little uncertain—"because of the, ah, nature of the alleged crime, you know, we thought Molly should come, too."

Jesse nodded.

"How about the girls?" Jesse said.

"That got, ah, checked?" Suit said.

"Uh-huh."

"I guess they're in class," Suit said. "I haven't had time to do a lot of investigating. Me and Eddie had our hands full with the parents."

Jesse nodded.

"Isn't this swell," he said.

Suit shrugged.

Jesse walked down the corridor to the lobby. The crowd of parents was silent now, standing in angry vigil.

"Get them down to the auditorium,"

Jesse said to Suit. "Get the names of their daughters and ask the girls to go there, too. You need help, call Steve, tell him to send some."

"You gonna talk to Mrs. Ingersoll?" Suit said.

"Yep."

"Then you coming to the auditorium?" Suit said.

"Yep."

"You know what you're gonna tell the parents?"

"Not a clue," Jesse said.

# 2

Jesse brought Molly with him when he went into Mrs. Ingersoll's office.

"Chief Stone," Mrs. Ingersoll said when he came into her office. "How lovely to see you. And this is?"

"Officer Crane," Jesse said.

"How do you do, Officer Crane," Mrs. Ingersoll said.

Molly nodded.

Mrs. Ingersoll smiled brightly.

"Have you dispersed those foolish people?" she said.

"We've asked them to wait in the

auditorium," Jesse said. "And we'll ask their daughters to join them there."

"My goodness," Mrs. Ingersoll said.

"Tell me about this situation," Jesse said.

Mrs. Ingersoll was sitting behind her big desk. The desktop was immaculately empty.

"Situation? Chief Stone, I fear that it overstates things to call it a situation."

"Tell me something," Jesse said.

"I have very little to tell," Mrs. Ingersoll said. "I'm not angry at these parents. They are concerned with their children's well-being, as am I."

Jesse waited. Mrs. Ingersoll smiled at him. Jesse waited. Mrs. Ingersoll smiled.

"The girls say you picked up their skirts and checked their underwear."

Mrs. Ingersoll continued to smile.

"Did you?" Jesse said.

Still smiling, Mrs. Ingersoll leaned forward and folded her hands on her desk.

"I have given twenty years of my life to this school," she said, "the last five as principal. Most people don't like the principal. Being police chief, you may understand. The students think I'm here to discipline them.

The teachers think I am here to order them about. Actually, of course, I am here to see to the well-being of the children."

Jesse nodded slowly. When he spoke his voice showed no sign of impatience.

"Did you look at their underwear, Mrs. Ingersoll?"

"I have done nothing illegal," she said brightly.

"Actually," Jesse said, "that's not your call, Mrs. Ingersoll."

Her eyes were big and bright. Her smile lingered.

"It's not?"

"You've been accused of an action," Jesse said pleasantly, "which, depending on the zeal of the prosecutor, the skill of the defense, and the political inclinations of the judge, might or might not be deemed a crime."

"Oh, Jesse," she said. "That's absurd."

"Did you check their undies, Betsy?" Jesse said.

She continued to smile. Her eyes continued to sparkle. But she didn't speak.

"Would you care to come down to the auditorium with me and thrash this out with the kids and their parents?" Jesse said.

"Try to keep this from turning into a hair-ball?"

She remained cheerfully motionless for a moment. Then she shook her head.

"Do you know who my husband is, Jesse?" she said.

"I do," he said.

"Well, I'm going to call him now," she said. "And I'd like you to leave my office, please."

Jesse glanced at Molly. Molly's lips were whistling silently as she stood studying the view from the window behind Mrs. Ingersoll. He looked back at Mrs. Ingersoll.

Then he said, "Come on, Moll, let's go talk to the girls."

As they left the office, Mrs. Ingersoll picked up the phone and began to dial.

# 3

"I'd like to drag her down to the station and strip-search her," Molly said. "Give her a little taste."

Jesse smiled.

"That option remains available, Moll," Jesse said. "But we probably need to talk to the victims first."

"I know," Molly said, "I know. But if it were one of my kids . . ."

The auditorium was subdued, as if the parents and the children were a little frightened by the circumstance they'd created. It was a small auditorium. Jesse sat on the lip of the stage.

"I'm Jesse Stone," he said. "I'm the chief of police. We can do this several ways. I can talk to you all, together, right here. Officer Molly Crane and I can talk to the girls separately, alone, or separately with a parent"—he grinned at the scatter of fathers—"or parents."

A hard-faced woman with brittle blond hair and a dark tan sat next to her daughter in the front row. She put up her hand. Jesse nodded at her.

"What does Ingersoll have to say?" she asked.

"Mrs. Ingersoll has neither affirmed nor denied anything," Jesse said. "So I thought I'd ask you."

The parents and children sat still in the auditorium. Eddie Cox and Suit leaned against the wall. Molly stood beside Jesse, resting her hips against the stage.

"Would one of the girls who were, ah, examined, like to tell us about it?" Jesse said.

The daughter of the brittle blonde looked down and didn't say anything. Her mother poked her. She continued to look down and shake her head.

"Me."

Jesse saw her, in the middle of the third row, a dark-haired girl, just developing a cheerleader's body if all went well.

"What's your name?" Jesse said.

She stood up.

"Bobbie Sorrentino," she said.

"Okay, Bobbie," Jesse said. "Is that your mother with you?"

"Yeah," Bobbie said, and nodded at her mother. "Her."

"Okay," Jesse said. "Tell me about it."

"I gotta stand?"

"Nope, stand, sit, up to you."

"I'm gonna stand," she said.

Jesse nodded.

"They got this stupid Wednesday-afternoon dance," Bobbie said. "You know, keep the kids off the street. Teach them manners."

She snorted at the thought. Several of the girls giggled.

"But if you don't go and everybody else goes, you feel like a dweeb, so we all go."

Jesse smiled.

"And the boys went," Jesse said.

"Yeah," Bobbie said, "sure."

Jesse nodded.

"I remember," he said.

Bobbie stared at him a moment, as if it had never occurred to her that Jesse had ever been in junior high.

"You go here?" Bobbie said.

"No, Arizona," Jesse said. "But school is pretty much school."

Bobbie nodded.

"So, before the dance," Bobbie said, "Old Lady Ingersoll lines us up and marches us into the girls' locker room and starts checking us out."

"What did she do," Jesse said.

"She picked up my skirt," Bobbie said, "and looked at my panties."

There was a small, uneasy stir in the crowd of kids and parents.

"She tell you why she did that?" Jesse said.

"She said"—Bobbie lowered her voice in mimicry—"'Proper attire includes what shows and what doesn't.'"

"Did she say what would have been improper?" Jesse said.

"She said anyone wearing a thong should leave now, because they'd be sent home if she saw one," Bobbie said.

"Anyone leave?" Jesse said.

"Couple girls," Bobbie said.

"Thongs?" Jesse said. "Or silent pro-
test?"

His face was perfectly serious. Bobbie
grinned at him.

"Or nothing," she said.

Most of the girls giggled.

"That'd probably be even more improper,"
Jesse said.

Some of the mothers joined in the gig-
gle.

"Anyone object to the, ah, panty patrol?"
he said.

"I did," Bobbie said, "and a couple other
girls, Carla for one, and Joanie."

"And Mrs. Ingersoll said?"

"She said it was all between us girls,
and she was trying to save us from being
embarrassed, if somebody saw."

Jesse took in a deep breath and let it
out.

He said, "How old are you, Bobbie?"

"I'll be fourteen in October."

"Thank you," Jesse said. "Anyone have
anything to add? Carla, Joanie?"

No one said anything.

"Parents?"

One of the fathers got to his feet. He was a husky guy, with the look of someone who worked outdoors.

"Can you arrest her?" the man said.

"What's your name, sir?"

"Charles Lane," he said.

"I'm not sure quite what the charge would be, Mr. Lane," Jesse said. "Molestation generally requires sexual content. Assault generally includes the intent to injure. There might be something about invasion of privacy, but I don't know that it would hold."

"We are not going to let this go," he said.

"No, sir," Jesse said. "I wouldn't if I were you."

"So what would you do?"

"I am going to talk to someone from the Essex County DA's office," Jesse said.

"You think we should get a lawyer?" Lane said.

Jesse grinned.

"That's pretty much what I'm doing," Jesse said.

# 4

Jesse had made sangria. He and Jenn sipped some as they sat together on the small balcony off his living room, looking at the harbor. It was early on a Saturday evening. Jenn had brought Chinese food, which was still in the cartons, staying warm on a low temperature in Jesse's oven.

"You know," Jenn said, "I realized the other day that we've been divorced longer than we were married."

"Yes," Jesse said.

"And yet, here we are."

"Yes," Jesse said.

Jesse had made the sangria in a large

glass pitcher, with a lot of ice. It sat on the low table between them, the condensation beading on the pitcher and making small tracks down the glass.

"I can't imagine life without you in it," Jenn said.

"Can't live with them," Jesse said. "Can't live without them."

"There are people who are doing worse than we are," Jenn said.

It was still daylight, and Jesse could see several people in rowboats scattered around the inner harbor, bottom-fishing for flounder. Jesse drank some sangria.

"And some doing better," Jesse said.

"Yes," Jenn said, "of course."

In one of the rowboats a young boy hooked a fish and hauled it in hand over hand. His father helped him take it off the hook.

"Is everything all right, Jesse?" Jenn said.

"It never is, Jenn," Jesse said.

He drank some sangria.

"But it's not worse than usual?" Jenn said.

Jesse looked at her and smiled.

"That might be our motto," Jesse said. "It's not worse than usual."

Jenn nodded.

"Are you seeing anyone these days?" she said.

"Several people."

"Anyone special?"

"They're all special," Jesse said.

"Because they have sex with you?"

"Exactly," Jesse said.

"Am I special?" Jenn said.

"Yes," Jesse said. "Even when we don't have sex."

"Is anyone else special like that?"

"No."

They were quiet for a time, drinking sangria, as the sun went down and the small boats came into the dock, and the lights went on in the boats moored in the harbor, and across the harbor in the houses on Paradise Neck.

"Maybe we should think about supper," Jenn said.

"Sure," Jesse said.

"We could eat out here," Jenn said.

Jesse nodded.

"You gonna spend the night, Jenn?"

"If I may," Jenn said.

"You may."

"I think we should have sex before we eat," Jenn said. "I do so much better on an empty stomach."

"You do well in any condition," Jesse said.

"Does it make me especially special?" Jenn said.

"One of the many things," Jesse said.

# 5

The ADA was a tall, athletic-looking woman named Holly Clarkson. Like a lot of assistant prosecutors, she was young, maybe five years out of law school, and earning some experience in the public sector before she sank comfortably into some law firm somewhere as a litigator.

"You want to arrest the principal of the junior high school?" Holly said. "And charge her with what?"

Holly always wore oversized round eyeglasses as a kind of signature. Today she was dressed in a beige pantsuit and a black shirt with long collar points.

"Whatever you can come up with," Jesse said.

"And you actually want to put her in jail?"

"Yes."

"You do know that her husband is the managing partner of the biggest law firm in the state," Holly said.

"Jay Ingersoll," Jesse said. "Cone, Oakes, and Baldwin."

"Correct," Holly said. "And she is accused of picking up the skirts of some junior-high girls and checking their underwear."

"Yes."

"That's idiotic," Holly said.

"It is," Jesse said.

"I admit," Holly said, "that it would be fun to see her do a little time, get her attention, so to speak."

"It would be," Jesse said.

"But you can't arrest somebody because it would be fun," Holly said.

"I can't?"

"No," Holly said. "And if we started prosecuting people for being idiotic . . ."

"Be a hot one for the press and the talk shows," Jesse said. "Elevate your profile."

"I'm not that ambitious," Holly said. "And

if I were, the approval of Jay Ingersoll would be more valuable to me than anything the press could give me."

"You got kids?" Jesse said.

"Not yet," Holly said. "First I need to get married."

Jesse nodded.

"Sure," Holly said. "I know if it were my kids I'd want to strangle the bitch. But to prosecute her for . . . whatever we come up with, and get buried in paper by a platoon of lawyers from Cone, Oakes. You know what they've got for resources?"

"More than Essex County?" Jesse said.

"More and better. Not everybody on staff in our office is a legal eagle like me."

"Anybody in your office got a death wish?" Jesse said.

"No," Holly said. "And if they did, Howard would fire them before they got a chance to enact it."

"The DA doesn't want to start anything," I said.

"The DA wants to get reelected next year," Holly said.

"How about by being tough on crime?"

"When people say that, they mean tough

on street crime. And tough on scary black kids with tats. They do not mean tough on annoying school administrators," Holly said.

"These are thirteen-year-old girls," Jesse said.

"Oh, please," Holly said. "I've been a thirteen-year-old girl, Jesse. They aren't adults, but they aren't innocent babies, either. You know as well as I do that thirteen-year-old girls can be sexually active."

"And why is that the school's business," Jesse said. "What happened to readin' and writin'?"

"Parents dump it on the schools," Holly said. "'Where were you when my Melinda was bopping little Timmy behind the back stop?'"

"And the panty patrol is supposed to prevent that?"

"Of course it won't," Holly said. "But Mrs. Ingersoll is, after all, an educator."

Jesse nodded.

"I never liked school," he said. "But in fact this may not be a problem with schools. This may be a problem with Mrs. Ingersoll."

"It may," Holly said.

"She shouldn't get away with it," Jesse said.

"Shouldn't?" Holly said. "You and I don't live in a world of should and shouldn't, Jesse."

Jesse grinned at her.

"I know," he said. "But we should."

# 6

Molly brought Missy Clark into Jesse's office. Missy was wearing running shorts and a cropped T-shirt and cowboy boots. There was dark makeup around her eyes, and a big gold hoop in her right ear. She was thirteen. Jesse gestured her to a chair. Molly lingered in the doorway.

"What can I do for you?" Jesse said.

Missy sat and looked at Jesse, then looked at Molly, and back at Jesse.

"I gotta talk to you alone," Missy said finally.

Jesse nodded.

"Officer Crane normally stays when

there's a woman alone with me in the office. Prevents misunderstandings."

"Misunder—? Oh," Missy said. "No. You're not like that."

Jesse smiled.

"That's right," he said. "I'm not."

He nodded at Molly and she went away. Missy looked at the open door.

"You may close the door if you'd like," Jesse said.

Missy got up and looked out into the corridor to see that Molly wasn't lurking there. Then she closed the door and went back to her chair. Jesse clasped his hands behind his head and leaned back in his chair.

"So," he said. "What's up."

"I saw you at school the other day," she said.

"Yes," Jesse said. "I saw you, too. Second row, at the far end to my right. Wearing a yellow sundress with small blue flowers on it. You didn't seem to be with your parents."

"Mrs. Ingersoll won't let us wear jeans or anything," Missy said. "How come you noticed me."

"I'm the chief of police," Jesse said. "I notice everything."

"You were nice to us," Missy said. "You were nice to Bobbie Sorrentino, when she talked."

"Why shouldn't I be nice to you?"

"'Cause we're kids and she's the principal."

Jesse nodded.

"You came along to that meeting even though your parents weren't with you," Jesse said.

"I didn't like that she made me pull my dress up," Missy said.

"Don't blame you," Jesse said.

Missy looked around the office. Jesse waited. Missy studied the picture of Jenn that sat on top of the file cabinet to Jesse's left.

"That your wife?" she said.

"Ex-wife," Jesse said.

"How come you got divorced?" Missy said.

Jesse smiled at her.

"None of your business," he said.

Missy nodded.

"She fool around?" Missy said.

"Answer stands," Jesse said.

"I was just wondering," Missy said.

Jesse nodded. He smiled at her again.

He said, "The way this usually works, Missy, is the cop asks the questions."

Missy nodded. Neither of them spoke for a time. Missy looked again at Jenn's picture.

"Is she that reporter on Channel Three?" Missy said.

Jesse didn't answer.

"She is. I seen her lots of times," Missy said.

Jesse waited. Missy looked around the office some more.

"I gotta tell you something," Missy said.

"Okay."

"You can't tell anybody," Missy said.

"Okay."

"You can't tell anybody I even talked to you," Missy said.

"Okay."

"You gotta promise," Missy said.

"Sure," Jesse said. "I promise."

"Even if I told you something like a murder or something, would you still not tell?"

Jesse shook his head.

"I'd tell," he said.

"Well, it's not a murder."

"Good," Jesse said.

"And I trust you," Missy said.

"Thank you," Jesse said.

They were quiet. Missy seemed to be gathering herself.

"I . . ." She stopped and took a breath and started again.

"You know what swinging is?" she said.

"As in the swinging lifestyle?" Jesse said.

"Yes . . . you know, wife-swapping."

"I know what that is."

Missy was silent. Jesse waited.

"My mom and dad do it," she said.

"Swing?"

"Yes."

"How do you know?" Jesse said.

"They have a swinger party about once a month at our house."

"And you've seen them," Jesse said.

"Me and my little brother are supposed to stay upstairs."

"But you peek," Jesse said.

"Yes."

"How old's your brother?"

"Eight," Missy said.

"Your parents know you know?"

Missy shook her head. Jesse took in a deep breath.

"How do you feel about it?" Jesse said.

"How would you feel?" she said. She looked as if she might cry.

"Awful," Jesse said.

Missy nodded.

"And my little brother," she said. "I mean, he's doesn't even exactly know what having sex is."

"It scare him?" Jesse said.

"Yes," Missy said. "How did you know that."

"Remember what I said about being chief of police," Jesse said.

Missy smiled faintly.

"You know everything?" Missy said.

"Exactly."

"That's how you knew we peeked," Missy said.

"Actually," Jesse said, "I knew that because that's what I woulda done."

Missy nodded.

"Most adults aren't like you," Missy said.

"Is that good or bad," Jesse said.

"Most grown-ups act like they were never a kid, you know?"

"Your parents like that?" Jesse said.

"Yeah. Do this. Do that. Be a lady. Blah, blah, and look at them. Look at what they're doing."

"Hard," Jesse said.

"Can you make them stop?" Missy said.

"As far as I know, there is no law against swinging," Jesse said.

"But it's wrong," Missy said. "You're not supposed to be like that if you're married, are you?"

"Probably not," Jesse said.

"So can't you tell them to stop it?"

"I can, but I can't force them," Jesse said. "And I assume you don't want them to know you blew the whistle."

"Oh, Jesus, no."

"So I'm not sure what I can do," Jesse said.

"So, okay, the hell with them. If they can live like that, so can I."

"If you actually want to," Jesse said, "I suppose you can. But revenge is a lousy reason for having sex."

Missy was silent again.

Then she said, "I don't really want to. It seems so icky."

"Scare you?" Jesse said.

"No . . . yes. I guess so."

"Why don't you wait until it doesn't," Jesse said.

"But what about my parents? Isn't there something you can do?"

"I'll think on it," Jesse said. "And maybe get some advice, without mentioning any names."

"Advice from who?"

"Oh, a shrink I know, maybe."

"I don't want to see no shrink," Missy said.

"I'm not asking you to. I see him, and I can ask him for advice."

"You see a shrink?" Missy said.

"I do," Jesse said.

"Is it about her?" Missy said, looking at Jenn's picture. "I bet it's about her. Is it?"

Again, Jesse smiled at her.

Again, he said, "None of your business."

# 7

Jay Ingersoll came into Daisy Dyke's at three-ten in the afternoon and spotted Jesse sitting at the counter. He walked over.

"Chief Stone," he said. "I'm Jay Ingersoll."

"How do you do," Jesse said.

Ingersoll was tall and lean, with thick white hair cut short and a dark tan. His dark summer suit fit him well, and he looked to Jesse like a man who probably played a lot of tennis.

"Mind if I join you?" Ingersoll said.

Jesse gestured at the stool next to him.

Ingersoll sat. He had small handsome character wrinkles around his eyes, and deep parenthetic grooves at the corners of his mouth.

"Apple pie?" Ingersoll said.

"Um-hm," Jesse said.

"Looks good," Ingersoll said.

"Daisy makes a nice pie," Jesse said.

"Was time, when I was your age," Ingersoll said, "I could have pie in the middle of the afternoon and still stay in shape."

"Sometimes I have two pieces," Jesse said.

The young woman behind the counter came down and Ingersoll ordered black coffee. When it came, he stirred in two packets of Splenda.

He raised the cup toward Jesse and said, "Cheers."

Jesse raised his empty fork in response, and Ingersoll sipped some coffee.

"Whoa," he said. "Hot."

"Often is," Jesse said.

Jesse noticed that Ingersoll's cheeks dimpled when he smiled.

"I'm Betsy Ingersoll's husband," he said.

"I know," Jesse said.

"I just wanted to tell you that I thought

you handled that incident at the school like a pro," Ingersoll said. "No press. Nothing blown out of proportion."

Jesse patted his mouth with his napkin.

"I am a pro," he said.

"I assumed you've closed the file on it," Ingersoll said.

"Um-hm," Jesse said.

"Um-hm what?" Ingersoll said.

"Um-hm, I hear what you're saying."

"And my assumption is correct?"

"No."

"You haven't closed the case," Ingersoll said.

"Not yet," Jesse said.

"For God's sake, why not?" Ingersoll said. "There's no crime here."

"Haven't found one yet," Jesse said. "I figure there'll be some civil action."

"And if there is?" Ingersoll said.

"I thought I'd watch," Jesse said. "See what I could see."

The lines around Ingersoll's mouth deepened.

"What the hell are you after, Stone?"

"You representing her?"

"I'm her husband, for crissakes."

"And her lawyer?" Jesse said.

"Whether or not I personally represent her," Ingersoll said, "you can be sure my firm will be involved."

"Rita Fiore?" Jesse said.

"She's a criminal litigator," Ingersoll said. "How do you know Rita?"

"I'm the chief of police," Jesse said. "I get around."

"You see this as your big chance?" Ingersoll said. "Make a name? Make some money? What's this about?"

"I think your wife violated those girls' rights," Jesse said.

"Oh, for crissakes, Stone."

"You asked," Jesse said.

"Would I have done it?" Ingersoll said. "No, I suppose not. Betsy is probably a little more, ah, authoritarian than I am, I guess. It's no easy job being a school administrator."

"Uh-huh."

"But no harm was done. No one was injured. No crime was committed," Ingersoll said.

"So you say."

"I have, of course, talked with Howard

Hannigan about this," Ingersoll said, "and he assures me that his office has no interest in pursuing the incident."

"I'm sure he doesn't," Jesse said.

"But you do," Ingersoll said.

"I'm not ready to clear it," Jesse said.

Ingersoll was silent for a moment. Then, with his hands folded tightly on the counter, he leaned toward Jesse a little.

"You are a small-town policeman," Ingersoll said. "You were fired from your last job. I am the managing partner of the biggest law firm in the state. If you continue to be an annoyance, I will bury you."

"No doubt," Jesse said.

He laid a five-dollar bill on the counter, and stood and walked out of the restaurant.

# 8

It was Wednesday night. It was his time. And the Night Hawk was beginning to dress. Black jeans, black socks, black sneakers. He put on a white T-shirt, and over it a black windbreaker, which he wore unzipped. He put on a navy-blue baseball cap, and pulled it low over his forehead, and looked at himself in the mirror. His beard covered the lower half of his face, and with the bill of the cap down low over his forehead he would be hard to recognize. He nodded to himself and reset the cap on the back of his head. Then he turned out the lights in his bedroom and went down the stairs and out the back door. He walked past Daisy's Restaurant, on down toward the water, past the Gray Gull and up Water Street. With no one in sight, he turned suddenly into a narrow alley just past the Paradise Inn. In the alley he zipped up his black windbreaker and pulled his baseball cap down over his forehead, then moved down the alley and into a scraggle of trees behind the inn. Past the trees was the harbor. The Night Hawk stood nearly invisible among the trees and looked into a first-floor bedroom at the back of the inn. The shade was up. The lights were on, but there was no one in the room. *I can wait,* the Night Hawk thought, and stood just outside the window. *Stolid, stoic, silent, and unseen.* The strong smell of the harbor drifted past him on the quiet evening air. The trees he stood among were white pine, and they added their pleasant scent to the night. Faintly from the inn came kitchen sounds, a hint of television, some barely audible music. The net effect was to emphasize the quiet. He looked at his watch. *I'll give it forty-five minutes,* the Night Hawk thought. He stood perfectly still, wrapping himself in the darkness. It was so still in the darkness that he could hear his own breathing. His breathing felt deep and quiet to him. He felt as if his heart was strong and his senses were keen. As if he could almost taste life in its full range and richness. The bedroom door opened and a woman came in. She was maybe fifty, with red hair and angular black glasses. *She'll do,* the Night Hawk thought. He felt the pressure, as if his interior were straining against the containment of his exterior. The woman was wearing tan slacks and a dark green top. She walked to the window and looked out. She was maybe two feet from him. He breathed very softly. She touched her hair, and the Night Hawk realized she wasn't looking out; she was studying her reflected self in the dark glass. He held his ground. Then she reached up and pulled the shade. He stayed steady, looking closely to see if the shade fully obscured the window. It didn't quite, but it allowed only a narrow view of a corner of the room, where a table stood. He watched to be sure. But she didn't go to the table, and after a while the lights went out. The Night Hawk shrugged and moved back down the alley toward Water Street. Before he stepped out of the alley, he tilted his cap to the back of his head and unzipped the black windbreaker so that the white T-shirt gleamed in the dim light from the streetlamps. He looked at his watch. *The night is young,* he said to himself, and started up Water Street like a watchman making his rounds.

# 9

Jesse sat with Suitcase Simpson in Jesse's unmarked car parked on an affluent street on the west shore of Paradise, where, on very clear days, from the second floor of certain homes, one could look north and see Cape Ann.

"Three doors up on the right," Jesse said. "Big garrison colonial with the fieldstone front."

"Yeah?" Suit said.

"That's the Clark house."

"Okay," Suit said.

"My information is that at regular intervals

they gather a number of couples together in that house and swap wives."

"Here?" Suit said. "In Paradise?"

"Incredible, ain't it," Jesse said.

"Unthinkable," Suit said.

"I have it on good authority," Jesse said.

"And you want me to go undercover," Suit said.

"Be more convincing if you had a wife," Jesse said.

"Well, maybe Molly—"

"Stop it," Jesse said.

Suit grinned. "So what do we care that they're banging their brains out in there?" he said. "Ain't illegal, is it?"

"Not that I know," Jesse said.

"So?"

"You know the Clarks?" Jesse said.

"I don't know, what're the first names?"

"He's Chase. She's Kimberly."

"Kimberly Magruder?"

"Yes."

"I went to school with her younger sister, Tammy," Suit said. "Tammy was pretty hot."

"And you know that how?" Jesse said.

Suit grinned again. "Hey," he said. "I was a football hero in high school, remember?"

"I remember you telling me," Jesse said.

"I cut a pretty wide swath in my letter sweater," Suit said.

"I'll bet you did," Jesse said. "You know Kimberly?"

"Just to say hi."

"Know anything about her?"

"I know she still looks pretty good," Suit said.

"Still? For crissakes, Suit," Jesse said. "She's not even forty yet."

"I'd give her a shot," Suit said.

Jesse nodded.

"Wear your football jersey," Jesse said. "How about the husband?"

"He played, but before I did," Suit said. "I think he's some kind of big-deal advertising guy in Boston now."

"I want you to find out everything you can about him, and about her, and about their social life."

"You mean the wife-swapping?" Suit said.

"They probably call it the swinging lifestyle," Jesse said.

"Course they do," Suit said. "But why do we care?"

"Their daughter came to me about it."

"Jesus, the daughter?" Suit said. "How old is she?"

"Thirteen," Jesse said, "I would guess."

"And she knows?"

"She knows," Jesse said. "And so does her eight-year-old brother."

Suit was quiet, looking down the street at the handsome house behind its smooth green lawn.

"Okay," he said. "It's awful, but what can we do about it."

"Not much," Jesse said. "Maybe something with children's services, but I kind of promised the daughter I wouldn't tell."

"You told me?"

"You don't count," Jesse said.

Suit grinned again.

"That ain't what Tammy Magruder used to say."

"For the moment," Jesse said, "we learn as much as we can. I mean, it's possible, you know, that the kid made it up."

"Thirteen?"

Jesse looked at him.

Suit nodded.

"Yeah," he said. "I withdraw the question."

# 10

"Oh, Jesse," Jenn said on the phone. "I'm so excited. I've got an offer in New York."

"New York," Jesse said.

"A new show called *Early On*," Jenn said. "I'd do weather, and some lifestyle stories."

"You gonna take it?"

"Oh, I have to. I mean, it's a huge jump up for me," Jenn said. "The show is syndicated, and looks like it'll go national in a while."

"So when do you leave?"

"I start on air next Monday," Jenn said.

"You got a place to live?"

"Well, I'll stay with a friend," Jenn said. "Until I find a place."

"Friend?"

"A guy friend."

"Anyone I know," Jesse said.

"I don't think so. He used to be up here, at Channel Three, and now he's producing *Early On*."

"That how you got the job?"

"Well, they were looking for somebody, and Rick thought of me."

"I'll bet he did," Jesse said.

"Oh, Jesse," Jenn said. "You're not going to go all jealous on me, are you?"

"Not me," Jesse said.

"I mean, you know, you left me," Jenn said, "when we first broke up."

"I did," Jesse said.

"I'll stay in touch," she said. "I promise."

"Okay," Jesse said.

"I will. I'll call you. We can e-mail. I don't want to lose touch with you, Jesse."

"I'll be standing by," Jesse said.

"You can call me on my cell," Jenn said. "If you need to."

"Sure," Jesse said.

"Well, I gotta get organized. Monday is coming quick."

"Yep."

"Wish me luck, Jesse?"

"Always," Jesse said.

They hung up. Jesse sat back a little in his chair and stared at nothing in the empty room. They weren't married anymore. She had a right to go where she wanted and to fuck who she wanted. His throat felt tight, and it was difficult to swallow. He stood and made himself a drink. Tall glass. Lot of ice. Couple of ounces of scotch. Fill with soda. He stood for a moment, stirring the drink with his forefinger. Behind the bar was a big picture of Ozzie Smith. Ozzie was in midair, parallel with the ground, stretched out as far as he could stretch, catching a line drive. Jesse nodded at the picture.

"Wizard," he said.

His voice sounded intrusive in the silent room. He took a drink of scotch.

"Best that ever played," Jesse said.

He drank some more scotch. He looked at the big bottle of scotch on the bar—1.75 liters. It was nearly full.

"I wouldn't have been that good," Jesse said. "But I'd have made the show. If I didn't get hurt, I'd have made the show."

He turned, carrying his glass, and walked across the living room. He stood and looked out the French doors at the harbor and began to drink his scotch.

# 11

It was becoming harder for the Night Hawk to wait for Wednesday night. He hadn't actually seen nakedness yet, but he'd seen women moving about in their bedrooms, unaware of being watched. If he kept his pace, sooner or later, he would see. Tonight he was in position to watch Lindsey Monahan through her bedroom window. There was a field behind her house, which you could reach by walking down the railroad tracks behind it. He lay flat in a low part of the field, behind a small outcropping of rock, with his binoculars. The light was on in her bedroom. But the room was empty. The Night Hawk was patient. Bagging the quarry was only the end part of a process. Like any hunt, the process was part of the pleasure. After an hour or so, Lindsey came into her bedroom. She took off her blouse, and her slacks. Her undergarments were red and frilly. *Lindsey is hotter than she seems,* the Night Hawk thought. She went into the bathroom and stayed there, out of sight for maybe ten minutes. When she came out of the bathroom she had a towel wrapped like a turban around her head, and was wearing a white terry-cloth robe that looked too big for her. *All spanking clean,* the Night Hawk said to himself. She came to the bed and sat, facing the window. The robe fell away a little over her knees, as the Night Hawk focused through his binoculars. He could feel his heart beat. She leaned sideways and turned off the light. *Damn.* The Night Hawk lay in position for a time, his binoculars ready. But the light didn't go on again. When he was sure it wouldn't, the Night Hawk stood and checked his watch, and walked back to the railroad tracks. *She sleeps naked,* he thought. He looked at his watch. Late. Too late to go to one of his other spots. He'd spent all evening on Lindsey and gotten to see her in her fancy underwear. That was something . . . but it wasn't enough.

# 12

Jesse had slept in his clothes and, despite a long shower, a pint of orange juice, three cups of coffee, and two aspirin, he still had a hangover. He was sipping his fourth cup, at his desk, when Molly Crane stuck her head in.

She said, "Two things, Jesse."

He nodded.

"We got a Peeping Tom report," Molly said. "And the DA is going to stop by here after lunch."

"Anything special about the peeper?" Jesse said.

"Nope. Some guy looking in a window,"

Molly said. "Ran off when the woman's husband yelled at him."

"Who's on patrol?" Jesse said.

"John Maguire and Arthur Angstrom," Molly said.

"Send John," Jesse said. "Howard Hannigan give a time?"

"I didn't talk to him," Molly said. "But his, ah, girl didn't specify exactly. Just 'after lunch.'"

"Wish I had a girl," Jesse said.

"You got me," Molly said.

"You're a woman," Jesse said.

"Well, I'm glad you noticed."

"Crow told me," Jesse said.

Molly blushed.

"Our secret, Moll," Jesse said.

"I certainly wish it were just mine," Molly said.

"Almost the same," Jesse said.

"I hope so," Molly said.

She studied Jesse for a moment.

"You're looking a little peaked today," she said.

"Drank more than I should have, last night," Jesse said.

"Alone?" Molly said.

"Yeah."

"Jenn?" Molly said.

"Yeah."

Molly took in a big breath of air and let it out slowly.

She said, "Might be time to move on, Jesse."

"Sure," Jesse said.

"If you can," Molly said.

"Sure," Jesse said.

"What's Dix say about it?"

"He seems to think I'm obsessed."

"You think so?" Molly said.

"Maybe I want to be obsessed."

"Maybe," Molly said.

Jesse didn't say anything else. Molly waited a moment in the heavy silence.

Then she said, "I'll send John down to talk to the Peeping Tom folks."

Jesse nodded. Molly stood for another moment, then turned and left the office. Jesse drank some coffee.

# 13

Howard Hannigan was thin-faced and dark-haired. He wore big horn-rimmed dark glasses, which he left in place when he came into Jesse's office.

"Jesse," he said. "We need to talk."

Jesse nodded and gestured Hannigan toward a chair.

"What's going on with Betsy Ingersoll?" Hannigan said.

"Nothing," Jesse said.

"So why is Jay Ingersoll telling me that you are persecuting his wife?"

"Don't know," Jesse said.

"Have you cleared the case?"

"No."

"Why not?" Hannigan said.

"Because she violated the civil rights of a number of thirteen-year-old girls, and I want there to be consequences for her."

"Consequences."

"Yep."

"So are you telling me," Hannigan said, "that you are leaving the case active to punish her?"

"Give her something to worry about," Jesse said. "Make her wish she hadn't done it."

"Jay has talked with you?"

"He has," Jesse said.

"And you know who he is?" Hannigan said.

"I do."

"I'm up for reelection this fall," Hannigan said.

"I know," Jesse said.

"In Jay Ingersoll's home county," Hannigan said.

"Yeah," Jesse said.

"It won't help me to have Jay mad at me."

"I can see how that would be," Jesse said.

"So you'll lay off his wife?" Hannigan said.

"Nope."

"You're willing to endanger my election? Just to annoy some goddamned school principal?"

"Yes, I am," Jesse said.

"For crissakes, Jesse. You don't have a prosecutable case."

"Yet," Jesse said.

"You mean you're still trying to get something more on her?"

"Yes, I am," Jesse said.

"Goddamn it, there's nothing to get. She embarrassed a few kids."

Jesse didn't say anything.

"Even if you came up with something," Hannigan said, "I wouldn't prosecute it."

Jesse didn't say anything.

"I've talked to the selectmen already," Hannigan said. "You want to get your ass in a crack, this is a good way to do it."

Jesse nodded.

"What the hell is wrong with you, Stone?" Hannigan said.

"You don't know, either?" Jesse said.

# 14

Jesse was sitting with John Maguire and Suit in the conference room at the station.

"What's up with the Peeping Tommy?" he said to Maguire.

"Nothing much," Maguire said. "Husband and wife"—he looked at his notes—"name of Richard and Alice North at Forty-one Rose Street, are getting ready for bed, bedroom's on the ground floor, when she looks out the window and sees some guy hiding in the bushes. Mr. North opens the window and yells at the guy and the guy scoots."

"That's it?"

"All they could tell me."

"Anything in the way of a description?" Jesse said.

"Nope, just an ordinary-sized guy dressed in dark clothes. They didn't see his face."

"He see anything?" Jesse said.

"The peeper?"

"Yes."

"Not as far as they told me. Why?"

"Just trying to find out whatever I can," Jesse said. "Sometimes with peepers what they see changes their future behavior."

"Really?" Maguire said.

Jesse nodded.

"Well," Maguire said. "They said they were getting ready for bed, but I thought Mrs. North looked a little embarrassed."

Jesse nodded.

"So maybe there was a little more going on than night-night," Suit said.

"Maybe," Maguire said.

"Peepers don't usually do anything more than peep, do they?" Suit said.

"Not usually," Jesse said. "But now and then they can escalate. Depends on what they see, sometimes, and how it affects them."

"I figure it's just some kid trying to see something he's never seen," Maguire said.

"Probably," Jesse said. "Stay on it, John, and any more calls are yours."

Jesse looked at Suit.

"How 'bout you?" Jesse said. "You got anything?"

Suit saluted smartly, and grinned.

"Paradise wife-swapping squad," Suit said. "Reporting."

"We got a fucking crime wave," Maguire said.

"It's called police work," Jesse said. "People report, we look into it. People complain, we check. You know?"

"Wife-swapping ain't even illegal," Maguire said. "Is it?"

"Kid complained," Jesse said. "Suit?"

"Well, they got a website," Suit said.

"Course they do," Jesse said.

Suit grinned.

"Call themselves a club, Paradise Free Swingers," he said. "They have parties, cookouts, outings. They go on trips. All celebrating the swinging lifestyle."

"Names?"

"Nope. Pictures of some members and

their first names. But I know a couple of them from school."

"In addition to Kimberly Magruder Clark?" Jesse said.

"Vinnie Basco. He played football with me in high school, wide receiver."

"Anybody else?"

"His wife," Suit said. "I think she was Debbie Lupo in high school."

"I'd love to be in a club like that," Maguire said.

"Wife-swapping?" Suit said.

"You bet," Maguire said. "As long as my wife isn't involved."

"I don't think it works that way," Jesse said.

"A shame," Maguire said.

Jesse grinned.

"Suit, can you talk to any of the people you know?" Jesse said.

"The guys, Clark and Basco," Suit said. "We were pretty tight, you know, playing football and all."

"See what you can find out," Jesse said.

"I don't even know what we want to find out," Suit said.

"Gives you plenty of room to maneuver," Jesse said.

# 15

The Night Hawk was tense. Last Wednesday he'd had his first big score. He'd seen her naked, making out with her husband. But they'd seen him and he'd had to run. It was sort of embarrassing to have to run off like that, like some pathetic little Peeping Tom kid. It had violated his autonomy, as the invisible watcher, taken away the power of his anonymity. But it had been sort of exciting as well, a little flirt of jeopardy that had intensified the Night Hawk's experience. As he dressed, the Night Hawk tasted the experience again, rolling it on the tongue, trying to discern it as if it were an expensive red wine. *It is like wine, in some ways,* the Night Hawk thought. *It's kind of intoxicating, the search, the possibility, the triumphant moment of total nudity in that woman's most intimate moment.* The Night Hawk wanted more. *It's rather like wine in that, too,* the Night Hawk thought as he started down the back stairs. *At least for certain kinds of drinkers, drinking makes you want to drink more. . . . I may be that kind of watcher. Maybe there is never enough.* As he walked through the darkness in the quiet town he could feel himself swell with importance, and tighten with uncertainty. Would he see her, any her, tonight, as he had last Wednesday? Would she be good-looking? A little plump? A little thin? Would she be younger, or old enough to show some gray? Sometimes women, after they undressed, had a little reddish indentation around their belly, where the elastic top of an undergarment had pressed into their skin.

He never went to the same part of town twice. Tonight he was in the commuter part of town, where they lived in rows of neat, expensive houses on quiet side streets. Halfway down such a street there was a cut-through to the next street, one that kids had probably worn. It was narrow, screened by bushes, and out of reach of the street-lights out front. The Night Hawk glanced around, saw no one, and turned into it. The land rose somewhat halfway along the cut-through, and at the top of the rise, if he stood up among the trees, the Night Hawk could see into the second-floor windows of the houses on Birch Avenue. At that place, the Night Hawk took up his vigil.

# 16

"I don't want to talk about myself today," Jesse said. "I need to talk a little bit about business."

"Sure," Dix said.

"You don't believe me?"

"Why would you lie to me?" Dix said.

"You shrinks ever give a direct answer?" Jesse said.

Dix smiled.

"Yes," he said.

Jesse nodded. Dix waited. His shaved head was shiny. His white shirt was bright. He seemed freshly showered and gleaming. Which was how he always looked.

"You hear about the school principal who made the girls show her their underwear?" Jesse said.

"I read a squib on it in the paper," Dix said. "I noticed it because it was in Paradise."

"I'm flattered," Jesse said.

Dix nodded his head once.

"Parents raised hell, we got called in . . ." Jesse shrugged. "What do you think of that?"

"Underwear surveillance?" Dix said.

"Yeah."

"I think it violated the civil rights of the girls," Dix said.

"Yeah," Jesse said, "I do, too."

Dix waited. His elbows were on his desktop. His thick hands were folded in front of his chin. He was perfectly still.

"I've had her in a couple of times," Jesse said. "Even if I've got no case against her, I at least want to make her uncomfortable."

Dix nodded.

"Her husband always comes with her," Jesse said. "You know who her husband is?"

"No," Dix said.

"Managing partner at Cone, Oakes, and Baldwin," Jesse said.

"Ah," Dix said.

"Ah is right," Jesse said. "DA won't prosecute and, in person, has told me to leave her alone. I've been admonished by the town selectmen not to bother her, also the chairman of the school committee."

"Has he supported the candidacy of these people?" Dix said.

Jesse smiled without humor.

"Oddly enough," Jesse said, "he has."

Dix nodded.

"But you can't let it go," Dix said.

"What will these kids think, if someone can violate their privacy like that and get away with it."

"Probably what they already think," Dix said.

"Even more reason," Jesse said. "And . . . and, goddamn it, I want to know why she did it."

"You've asked her," Dix said.

"Every time," Jesse said. "Sometimes she says she doesn't want them embarrassed if someone saw them."

"Which is why she made them publicly show what they were wearing?" Dix said.

"Uh-huh. I don't have kids," Jesse said. "So maybe I don't know. But my guess would be that the most embarrassed would be some kid wearing white cotton undies that her mother bought in a six-pack at Kmart."

Dix nodded.

"Last time we talked she said she was trying to keep them from becoming sluts when they got older," Jesse said.

Dix smiled.

"Would that it were that easy," he said. "She offer any other explanations?"

"Not really. As I said, her husband is always with her, and he doesn't let her talk much."

"Like any good attorney," Dix said.

"Yeah," Jesse said, "I know. He always accuses me of harassment and threatens to bring charges."

"So why have you told me this," Dix said.

"I don't know," Jesse said. "You got any thoughts?"

"There may be a civil action available to the parents," Dix said.

"Yeah."

"But you want more," Dix said.

"I want to know what she was really doing," Jesse said. "What do you think?"

Dix leaned back a little in his chair and put one foot against the edge of his desk. His shoes gleamed with polish.

"I agree with you that her avowed reasons are bullshit," Dix said.

"So what was she doing?"

"Acting out something we know nothing about," Dix said. "We don't know what her interior life is. We don't know what underwear means to her in that life. One reason she did what she did is that she could."

"You mean power," Jesse said.

"Yes. And we don't know where the connection is made between power and sluthood and underwear. Or why it's made."

"How do we find out?"

"We could have her come talk to me for a couple of years."

Jesse grinned.

"Her and her husband," Jesse said. "Who'd be telling her not to speak."

"You think he oppresses her in more than a lawyerly way?" Dix said.

"I don't know. He's an oppressive kind of guy."

"If he is, then you could throw that into the mix," Dix said.

"And then what have I got?" Jesse said.

"A mystery," Dix said, "wrapped in an enigma."

"So far," Jesse said.

# 17

"Got two more Peeping Tom reports," John Maguire told Jesse.

Maguire was a fitness guy. He did martial arts. He lifted weights. And he looked it.

"Any pattern?" Jesse said.

"No," Maguire said. "Not that I can see. One downtown, near the wharf. One up in the west end of town."

"Maybe he's making sure there is no pattern," Jesse said.

"That's sort of a pattern," Maguire said.

"Doesn't help us much," Jesse said.

"Seems to be getting more active, though," Maguire said.

"Or people are being more careful," Jesse said.

"Pretty much everybody in town knows there's a peeper on the loose," Maguire said. "Everybody's looking out their window."

"And reporting anybody they see," Jesse said.

"So some of these may not really be the peeper," Maguire said.

Jesse shrugged.

"Could even be a copycat," he said.

"Or several," Jesse said.

"Hell, we've practically got the cuffs on him," Maguire said.

"Stay with it, Johnny," Jesse said. "I got nobody to help you."

"It'll be luck," Maguire said. "We'll spot him by accident someplace. Or he'll look in the wrong house and somebody's husband will make a, ah, citizen's arrest."

"Be nice," Jesse said.

"Anyway," Maguire said. "All the women got to do is pull their shades."

"So far," Jesse said.

"I been reading up a little," Maguire said. "Peepers don't normally take it further."

"Not usually," Jesse said.

"On the Internet it says 'rarely.'"

"Sure," Jesse said.

"You're saying 'rarely' doesn't mean 'never'?"

"I got a twelve-man force here, and I've got you on this full-time," Jesse said.

"Because it's possible," Maguire said.

"Otherwise, he's just a nuisance."

"Yeah," Maguire said. "I'll keep on it."

"You've interviewed all the victims," Jesse said.

"Sure," Maguire said, "and wrote it up."

Jesse nodded.

"Interview them again," he said.

"They'll say the same thing," Maguire said.

"Usually people don't," Jesse said. "Maybe there's something they left out, forgot, dismissed as irrelevant. Their stories are all we've got, Johnny. You may as well keep working them."

"Okay, Jesse."

"And be polite and friendly," Jesse said. "We don't want them to wish they'd never reported it."

"I am always polite and friendly," Maguire said.

"I know that," Jesse said. "Course, there

was that guy fell down the stairs while in your custody."

"Accidents happen," Maguire said. "Besides, he was beating on his wife and kids."

Jesse nodded.

"And you would never throw somebody down a flight of stairs," Jesse said.

"Absolutely not, Chief."

Jesse nodded.

"That's what I told the selectmen," he said.

"Protect and serve," Maguire said.

"Absolutely," Jesse said. "I wonder if there are any people who've been peeped at and haven't reported it."

"Probably," Maguire said. "There usually are, I guess."

"See if you can find any," Jesse said.

"I'm on it," Maguire said.

"And if you find any," Jesse said, "try not to throw them down the stairs."

"God, Jesse," Maguire said. "You spoil everything."

Jesse grinned.

"It's how I got to be chief," he said.

# 18

Jesse met Rita Fiore after work at the bar in the Langham Hotel in Post Office Square. She was wearing a green-and-blue dress with a skirt that ended well above the knees. Her thick, red hair was down to her shoulders. She had on slingback stiletto heels. Jesse stood when she came to the bar.

"Still got the wheels," he said.

"Thanks for noticing," Rita said.

She slid onto a bar stool next to him.

"There a dress code at Cone, Oakes?" Jesse said.

"Yes," Rita said. "Otherwise, I'd dress sort of flamboyantly."

"If you were more flamboyant," Jesse said, "you'd get arrested."

"By you?"

"I'm out of my jurisdiction," Jesse said.

"Damn," Rita said.

She ordered a mojito.

"How's Jenn?" Rita said.

"Gone to New York," Jesse said.

"Alone?"

"No."

Rita sipped her mojito, looking at Jesse over the rim of the glass.

"So is that why we're having a drink?" Rita said.

"You mean, am I looking for backup?" Jesse said.

"Something like that."

"I asked you to meet me because I like you, and I like to see you, and I need some information from you."

"In that order?" Rita said.

Jesse smiled and drank a little of the beer he was nursing.

"No particular order," he said.

Rita nodded.

"I don't mind being backup," she said.

Jesse nodded.

"We'll return to that in a little while," he said. "First, I need to ask you about your managing partner."

"Jay?" she said.

"Uh-huh."

"Why do you want to ask me . . . oh! . . . his wife and the panty inspection."

"Yep."

"It happened in Paradise," Rita said.

"Yep."

"It's been very embarrassing for Jay."

"I'll bet it has," Jesse said.

"Are you still pursuing that?" Rita said.

"Sort of," Jesse said. "Nobody much wants me to."

"I'll bet that bothers you a lot."

Jesse shrugged.

"She violated those kids' civil rights," he said.

"I'm not sure that's a legally sustainable argument," Rita said.

"But she did."

Rita smiled.

"And you want her to suffer some consequence," she said.

"I do."

"That would be you," Rita said. "If it's any

consolation, Betsy Ingersoll is probably pretty embarrassed and wishes it hadn't happened."

"You know her?"

"Not really," Rita said. "She attends a few of the hideous social events the firm occasionally runs, to prove how warm and fuzzy we are. She doesn't get to say much."

"Because Jay does most of the talking?"

"Nearly all," Rita said.

"Okay," Jesse said. "So tell me about her husband."

"He was a hell of a lawyer," Rita said.

"Was?"

"He probably still is," Rita said. "But he doesn't do much law anymore. Now he mostly manages the firm."

"And the firm does well," Jesse said.

"Very," Rita said.

"He love his wife?" Jesse said.

"I don't know."

"Say he does," Jesse said. "What else does he care about?"

"The firm."

"Anything else? Kids?"

"No kids," Rita said.

Rita finished her mojito. The bartender stepped promptly over.

"Another one, Ms. Fiore?" he said.

"Yes."

"You, sir?" the bartender said. "Another beer?"

Jesse hesitated.

"Drink scotch, Jesse," Rita said. "You look miserable."

"Dewar's and soda," Jesse said to the bartender.

"Yes, sir."

Rita said, "Have you met Jay?"

"He came by and leaned on me a little bit," Jesse said.

"There are a lot of successful men like him," Rita said. "After a while he starts to think that he can do whatever he decides to do and who's to say nay."

"You like him?" Jesse said.

"I admire him," Rita said.

"Would you want to be married to him?" Jesse said.

"Oh, God, no," Rita said.

"Because?"

"He's totally self-absorbed, like so many of them."

"He appears to be protecting his wife," Jesse said.

"He's protecting his reputation," Rita said.

"He doesn't want to be seen as the husband of a dope."

Jesse nodded.

"Why are you so interested?" Rita said. "You going to take him on?"

"Just gathering information," Jesse said. "It's always better to know stuff."

"Well, he's got a lot of chits that he can call in," Rita said.

"I figured," Jesse said.

"And he'll call them if he needs to," Rita said. "Don't think he's just another empty suit."

"I won't," Jesse said.

"On the other hand," Rita said, "neither are you."

# 19

Everyone in town seemed to be interested in, or amused by, or frightened about, the Peeping Tom at large. They knew about him. They didn't know his name. But they knew what he did. The Night Hawk was scared . . . and titillated. He didn't make his usual rounds this Wednesday night. Instead, in civilian dress, he strolled around Paradise, getting a look at the way things were. Shades were down all over town. It made him smile and stirred some sense of power in him. There seemed to be no unusual police activity. No stakeouts, no

prowl cars driving slowly through the neighborhoods. The Night Hawk felt faintly dis-
appointed that there was no more police
activity. Wasn't much of a police department, anyway. And it was encouraging
that maybe he could still make his rounds.
But not the same way. No one would be
careless about their shades anymore . . .
unless he found an exhibitionist. *Wouldn't
that be a chuckle,* he thought, *for a voyeur
and an exhibitionist to find each other.* That
was pretty unlikely, he knew. And he also
knew without quite saying it that it wouldn't
work anyway. He didn't want to keep seeing them. He just wanted to discover their
secret and move on, and discover someone else's. Maybe he should work another
town for a while. Until things relaxed . . .
*No.* He didn't want things to relax, and he
preferred to discover his secrets in this
town. Where he lived. Where he knew
most of the people. He stopped at the
mainland end of the causeway to Paradise
Neck, and leaned his forearms on the top
of the wall, and looked at the ocean. It
would be awfully frustrating, night after
Wednesday night, to be unsuccessful. He
hadn't even seen a bedroom in the last

two weeks. Everywhere the shades were drawn. . . . There was no wind. The stars were high. The black ocean quietly murmured against the causeway. . . . He stared out to sea. . . . *Okay,* he thought. *A new venue. More risk, yes.* But the rewards were greater. He smiled to himself in the darkness. *Like the stock market,* he thought. *Bigger the risk, bigger the reward.*

# 20

Suit came into Jesse's office carrying a bag of doughnuts.

"Sex in Paradise," he said. "The saga continues."

He put the doughnuts down on the edge of Jesse's desk. Jesse took one out of the bag and had a bite.

"I got an expense account to submit," Suit said.

"For what?"

"I bought a few beers for Vinnie Basco," Suit said. "And I took Debbie Basco and Kim Clark for lunch."

"Give it to Molly," Jesse said.

Suit nodded and drank some coffee.

"You learn anything?" Jesse said.

"I bought Vinnie a few beers at the Gray Gull. I told him I was curious about the Paradise Free Swingers. You know, not as a police officer, just as a guy used to play ball with him."

"He buy that?" Jesse said.

"I don't think so. But his real problem was that he was embarrassed about it. Said it was kind of creepy."

"Then why does he do it?" Jesse said.

"My question exactly. And my answer to myself was"—Suit grinned—"the little woman."

Jesse nodded and fished another doughnut out of the paper bag.

"So I say to Vinnie," Suit went on, "'Your wife likes it?' And he says, 'Yeah, it turns her on.' And that's about all I got out of that. Rest of the time we talked about how if I coulda held my block longer he'd have had more time to run the deep patterns. And I say to him if he were faster I wouldn'ta had to hold my blocks so long. And like that. I always thought Vinnie was an okay guy."

"You talk with Chase," Jesse said.

"Chase Clark? Naw, he's an asshole. Always was. I couldn't stand him, and he couldn't stand me."

"Hard to believe," Jesse said.

"How I know he's an asshole," Suit said.

"So you went for the wives," Jesse said.

"I did. Kim Clark was ahead of me in high school. I guess I had kind of a crush on her."

"She show early promise?" Jesse said.

"As a future swinger?" Suit said. "No. But she did get knocked up. It's why she's got a thirteen-year-old daughter, and she's only a few years older than me."

"So maybe she did," Jesse said. "How about Debbie?"

Suit grinned.

"She showed a lot of promise," he said. "With about everybody."

"You had lunch with them together?"

"Yeah," Suit said. "They was always buddies, even when Kimmy was into being Catholic."

"And Debbie wasn't," Jesse said.

"Not so it showed. I told them I was investigating another case that had nothing to do with them, but that I needed to learn as much as I could about the swinging lifestyle."

"And they told you," Jesse said.

"Maybe more than I wanted to know," Suit said.

"Cocktails with lunch?" Jesse said.

"Line of duty," Suit said. "And a couple bottles of wine."

"Candy is dandy," Jesse said, "but liquor is quicker."

"Man," Suit said. "I never drink in the middle of the day. I barely sipped a little wine, and I had to go home and take a nap."

"Being a lush is heavy work," Jesse said. "What'd they tell you."

"Well, for openers," Suit said, "they talked about it like it was some kind of high-minded philosophy of life. The swinging lifestyle."

"Liberated," Jesse said.

"Yeah, 'free of prudish' . . . what did she say? 'Free of prudish limitations.' That's what Debbie told me," Suit said.

"Only a repressed pervert would disapprove," Jesse said.

"Debbie says that studies show that swingers have happier relationships and more stable marriages."

"Because they are open and loving, and there's no surreptitious nookie going on," Jesse said.

"Wow," Suit said. "Surreptitious nookie."

"I amaze myself, sometimes," Jesse said. "How's it work?"

"The swingers club?"

"Yep."

"Couples only," Suit said. "No single guys."

"Leaves us out," Jesse said.

"Yeah," Suit said. "Don't seem fair, does it?"

"How about single women?" Jesse said.

"No rules that I know of about that," Suit said.

"Sexist bastards," Jesse said. "So do they meet regularly?"

"They meet once a month at a club member's home," Suit said. "And they also have, you know, parties and cookouts and picnics, stuff like that."

"And this is all about partners having sex with other people's partners," Jesse said.

"I guess," Suit said. "I know that sometimes one partner watches while the other partner does it."

"I wonder how they decide," Jesse said.

"Who's gonna do what with who?" Suit said. "Yeah, I wondered about that."

"But you didn't ask," Jesse said.

"I was getting embarrassed," Suit said.

"Cops don't get embarrassed," Jesse said.

"Never?" Suit said.

Jesse grinned at him.

"Hardly ever," he said. "Debbie seems to have done most of the talking. What did Kim have to say?"

"Not much. She was kind of agreeing with Debbie, but I don't know. She didn't seem to have much to say about it."

"She's the one we should talk with," Jesse said.

"Because she didn't say much?"

"Be good to know why she didn't," Jesse said

# 21

Jesse sat at a table in Daisy's Restaurant and looked at Sunny Randall sitting across from him wearing tight jeans and a white tank top.

"Hard to carry a concealed weapon in that outfit," Jesse said.

"This outfit is not about concealing," Sunny said. "Gun's in my purse."

Jesse nodded.

"The outfit is doing its job," Jesse said.

"Of not concealing?"

"Yes."

"I was hoping you'd notice," she said.

They were drinking iced tea and eating

sandwiches. Sunny had a BLT. Jesse had a lobster club.

"We got an agenda on this visit?" Jesse said.

"You mean why did I come up here and have lunch with you?"

"Yes."

"How about because you're a white-hot stud, and I've missed you," Sunny said.

"Nice answer," Jesse said.

"It's true. I do miss you," Sunny said.

"Yes," Jesse said. "I miss you, too."

"And," Sunny said, "I want a favor."

Jesse nodded.

"Don't they always," Jesse said.

"Ohmigod, the weltschmerz," Sunny said.

"I'm trying it out," Jesse said. "How's it play?"

"Sucks," Sunny said. "Here's what I need."

Jesse smiled and nodded.

"You remember my friend Spike," she said.

"Sure, big guy, beard, looks sort of like a bear."

"That would be Spike," Sunny said.

She opened her sandwich and picked

up a slice of bacon and took a small bite off the end of it. Sunny always looked as if she'd recently stepped from the shower, combed her hair, applied her makeup carefully, and dressed. There was a freshness about her that made her seem always nearly brand-new.

"He owns a restaurant in Boston," Sunny said. "Spike's. Near Quincy Market."

"Clever name," Jesse said.

"He wants to expand," Sunny said. "And he's looking to get a place up here."

"Spike's North?" Jesse said.

"Yes," Sunny said, "in fact. How'd you know?"

"You got something really clever," Jesse said. "You probably like to work with it."

Sunny took a red lettuce leaf from her deconstructed sandwich and nibbled on it.

"I thought being down with the chief of police might be useful to him," she said.

"How useful has it been for you?" Jesse said.

"More than maybe you know," Sunny said.

They were quiet for a moment, waiting for the conversation to go to another place.

"I could put him in touch with my friend Marcy Campbell. She's a real estate broker."

"Good friend?" Sunny said.

"Yes."

"With privileges?" Sunny said.

"Why do you ask?" Jesse said.

Sunny nibbled on a tomato slice. Then she put it down and patted her mouth with her napkin.

"How's Jenn," she said.

"Gone to New York," Jesse said.

"To work?"

"Yes."

"She go by herself?"

"No."

"Man?" Sunny said.

Jesse leaned back in his chair and looked at the ceiling, as if he were stretching his neck.

After a time he said, "Of course."

Sunny nodded. She sipped some iced tea. Jesse sat forward and smiled at her.

"How's Richie?" Jesse said.

"I don't exactly know," Sunny said. "We decided to try a sabbatical from one another. I mean, you know, for God's sake, his current wife is having a baby soon."

Jesse nodded.

"And Rosie?"

Sunny shook her head.

"I had to put her down," she said. "This spring."

"Oh, God," Jesse said. "I'm sorry."

"I know," Sunny said. "I'll get past it."

"Hard," Jesse said.

"Very."

He put his hand on hers on the tabletop. They sat quietly. The waitress came and asked if they were interested in dessert. They said no. She brought them the check. Jesse paid it and added a tip.

"Let's get out of here," Jesse said.

"And go where?" Sunny said.

"We can start with a walk on the beach," Jesse said.

"That feels right," Sunny said.

"It does," Jesse said.

And they left the restaurant.

# 22

Eddie Cox called in.

"Jesse," he said. "I got a home invasion. I think you need to come down here, now, and bring Molly."

"Where," Jesse said.

Cox gave him the address on Beach Street.

"Here I come," Jesse said.

"Can we do the siren?" Molly said as they drove to Beach Street.

"No need," Jesse said.

"Damn," Molly said, and settled back in the passenger seat with her arms folded. "What are we going to?"

"Home invasion," Jesse said. "Must be a woman involved. Cox requested you."

"Maybe he just wanted my superior investigative skills," Molly said.

"Maybe," Jesse said.

Cox's patrol car was parked on the street in front of an ordinary-looking smallish white colonial-style house on a street of smallish colonials in the south part of town, near the commuter railroad station. There was a pear tree in the front yard.

When Jesse rang the bell, Cox opened the front door and gestured them to the living room, which ran the length of the house from back to front. A woman sat on the couch, wearing jeans and a white T-shirt. She was crying.

"Kids?" Jesse said.

Molly walked over and sat down on the couch beside the woman.

"In school," Cox said. "Husband works in Boston. He's on his way."

"Name?" Jesse said.

Cox glanced at his notebook.

"Dorothy Browne," he said.

Jesse nodded and walked to the couch.

"I'm Jesse Stone, Mrs. Browne. Are you okay?"

She nodded.

"Can you tell me what happened?" Jesse said.

She nodded again. Molly sat quietly beside her. Jesse waited. Mrs. Browne gathered herself.

"What if the kids had been here," she said.

"It's good that they weren't," Jesse said.

Mrs. Browne took a couple of breaths.

"Michael went to work like always, the seven-forty train from Preston Station. I got the kids onto the school bus at eight." She smiled very faintly. "That's always a struggle. I cleaned up breakfast dishes, made the beds, took a shower, and dressed for the day."

Across the room from where she sat on the couch was a small, clean fireplace, and above it a large oil painting of surf breaking over the kind of rock outcroppings that lined the coast north of Boston. She stared at it blankly as she talked. Her voice was under tight control, almost monotone.

"I came downstairs all neat and clean," she said, "with my makeup on, and he was in my living room with a ski mask on . . . I was going to have coffee and read the paper."

Eddie Cox stood near the front door, looking uneasy. Molly sat close to Mrs. Browne on the couch. Jesse waited.

"He had a gun," she said. "He said he wouldn't hurt me if I did what he said. I said, I think, something like 'What do you want?' He said for me to take off all my clothes."

Jesse nodded.

"So I said something really stupid like 'Why?' And he said, and I remember him saying it just like this, 'Because if you don't I will hurt you, but if you do, I won't.'"

She paused and hugged herself as if she were cold. Molly patted her arm gently.

"I couldn't seem to get started for a minute. I just stood there and he made a little gesture with the gun, and he said, 'You want me here when the kids come home from school?'"

Her eyes filled as if she was going to cry. But she didn't. She got under control again.

"So I undressed." She looked down at her lap and shivered. "He stood there and watched me take my clothes off. In my living room, at, like, ten o'clock in the morning."

Cox turned and looked out through the narrow glass sidelights flanking the front door. Molly continued to pat Mrs. Browne's arm.

"And when I got entirely naked, he just stood there looking at me. I think I said something like 'Please don't rape me.' And he nodded and took out one of those little digital cameras and took pictures of me."

"Oh, God," Molly said.

"I didn't know what to do. I just had to stand there. Then he told me to lie face-down on the couch and close my eyes and count to one hundred without looking up. . . . In some ways that was the worst; I didn't know what he would do. So I counted, and when I got through counting I sort of peeked and he was gone. And I sat up and he was still gone. So I put on my clothes and called you."

"How close did he get?" Jesse said.

"Close?"

"Uh-huh."

"Not very," Mrs. Browne said. "Not as close as you are now."

"So he didn't touch you," Jesse said.

"No."

Jesse looked around the living room. There were no pictures except the oil painting above the fireplace.

"How did he know you had kids?" Jesse said.

"I don't know," Mrs. Browne said.

"You didn't mention them?"

"No."

"You didn't recognize this man?" Jesse said.

"He was wearing a ski mask," she said. "I told you that."

"I know," Jesse said. "But sometimes people recognize a voice, or mannerisms, if the masked person is well known to them."

"I have no idea who this man was."

"Okay," Jesse said. "Couple of things. First, I am very sorry that this happened to you. I can't make it up to you. But I can try very hard to catch this guy."

Mrs. Browne nodded.

"Second, when your husband gets

home, you and he will need to decide what you're going to tell the kids, keeping in mind that this story may become public knowledge."

"What do you think he'll do with the pictures," Mrs. Browne said.

"I don't know," Jesse said. "Often they keep them to themselves."

"They?"

"People who do this sort of aggressive voyeurism," Jesse said.

"There are people who do this?" Mrs. Browne said.

"Yes."

"But they don't always keep the pictures to themselves?" Mrs. Browne said.

"No," Jesse said.

"Oh, God!"

"You and your husband should talk when he gets here," Jesse said.

Mrs. Browne nodded.

"The other thing," Jesse said. "Do you have a place where you could go for the rest of the day?"

"Kids, too?" she said.

"Yes, everyone, until about suppertime?"

"I guess we could go across the street," she said. "The Cronins. Why?"

"I want to seal the house off so my crime scene guy can go over it."

"There won't be any fingerprints," she said. "He was wearing those latex gloves, like doctors wear."

"Still need to go over the house," Jesse said. "If we may."

"Okay," she said.

"Officer Crane will go with you," Jesse said. "You and she can talk more."

"What if he comes back?" Mrs. Browne said.

"We'll see to it," Jesse said, "that you are not alone."

Mrs. Browne nodded.

"So," Jesse said. "Moll, why don't you take Mrs. Browne over to the Cronins', where you can talk."

Molly nodded.

"What about my husband?" Mrs. Browne said.

"We'll send him over when he gets here."

"Can you let me tell him," she said.

"Of course," Jesse said.

They were quiet.

Then Mrs. Browne said, "All he did was see me naked."

Molly said, "Yes."

"I'm forty-one," Mrs. Browne said. "Other men have seen me naked. Not a bunch, but some."

"Sure," Molly said.

"My body is still okay," Mrs. Browne said. "It's not like I should be ashamed of my body."

"Of course not," Molly said.

"So why is this such a big deal?" Mrs. Browne said.

Molly put her arm around Mrs. Browne's shoulders.

"It is a big deal," Molly said. "For you."

"Why?"

"The others were voluntary," Molly said.

# 23

Betsy Ingersoll came into Jesse's office and sat down in a chair in front of his desk and crossed her legs.

Betsy Ingersoll came into Jesse's office and sat down in a chair in front of his desk and crossed her legs.

*Not unattractive,* Jesse thought. *A little sturdy maybe, but not so sturdy that she was unattractive.*

"Thanks for coming in," Jesse said.

"You are the chief of police," Mrs. Ingersoll said. "I respect authority."

"Wish there were more like you," Jesse said. "May I call you Betsy?"

"Which is not to say I necessarily respect you."

"Just the office," Jesse said.

"Why do you wish to see me?" she said.

"I wanted to ask you a few more questions about the recent incident, Betsy," Jesse said. "Would you like to have your attorney present?"

"You mean my husband," Mrs. Ingersoll said. "I am capable of speaking without him."

"So you are willing to speak to me without counsel," Jesse said.

"I have done nothing wrong," she said. "I am willing to speak with anyone."

"Nice," Jesse said. "How many of the girls you checked on that day were inappropriately clothed?"

"How many?"

"Yeah, how many were too risqué, or whatever?" Jesse said. "Isn't that why you checked?"

"Chief Stone," Mrs. Ingersoll said. "That was some time ago now. I have no idea."

"You checked twenty-two girls," Jesse said. "Of whom you sent thirteen home to change."

"If you knew that, why did you bother to ask?"

"I'm a small-town police chief, Betsy. I got nothing else to do."

"I would prefer to be called Mrs. Ingersoll," she said.

"Ah, it's so formal," Jesse said. "You want to get even, call me Jesse."

"Do you have anything else?" Mrs. Ingersoll said.

"Of the thirteen you sent home to change, were all of them wearing thongs?"

"That is a preposterous question," she said.

"The whole business is preposterous, Betsy. How many were wearing thongs?"

"I have no idea."

"Seven thongs," Jesse said. "Four bikinis. And a couple that were too lacy, or the wrong color, or something."

"Undergarments are not ornamental," Mrs. Ingersoll said. "They are for sanitation and modesty."

"Does Victoria's Secret know about this?" Jesse said.

"You are badgering me, Chief Stone, pure and simple," Mrs. Ingersoll said. "And I don't know why."

"I'm trying to understand, Betsy."

"There is nothing to understand," she said. "My job is the well-being of those children. Not merely that they can read and write; my concern is the whole child, and I will not allow my girls to be anything less than ladies."

"Chilling," Jesse said.

"I beg your pardon?"

The door to Jesse's office was open, and Jay Ingersoll appeared in it.

"What the hell is going on here?" he said.

Jesse glanced up at him and smiled.

"Ah, Jay," Jesse said. "If only I knew."

# 24

The Night Hawk was frightened. He had gone way past what he'd ever thought he'd do. And he'd done it in broad daylight. Would he have forced her if she resisted? Would he have shot her? He looked at her picture on the computer screen. Naked and frightened. He clicked onto the other pictures of her. Why? They were essentially the same picture. Yet he felt compelled to look at each of them. And each time he felt the same fearful surge. The same tangle of desire and fright and unsated appetite. It was an uncompleted experience, he realized. And no matter how much he looked, it remained incomplete, and yet looking somehow compelled him to keep looking. . . . He felt shaky. He'd gotten away with it this time, no one had seen him. He'd been careful and left no trace. He should stop. He'd done it. And now he should give it up. All of it. The whole Night Hawk thing. It wasn't too late. He could have had this life and left it, and he could be safe . . . destroy these pictures, maybe even destroy the computer. Be perfectly safe. No one would ever know. . . . He stared some more at the naked, frightened woman whose name he didn't even know. . . . *I can't destroy the pictures. . . .* He clicked on the next one. Same woman. Same body. Same fear. *Why keep looking* . . . And just as he kept looking, he knew he'd do it again. He knew he'd scout carefully, observe another woman's home, get the lay of the land, and, when he was sure, and things were right, he'd go in and make her undress. Take her picture. Then he'd have her secret, in his computer, available to study, never quite enough. *I won't stop. Maybe I can't stop.*

*What if I do something worse? I don't want to do something worse. But what if I do?* He shook his head as if to clear it, and began to click through his pictures again.

# 25

"You have no business talking to my wife without me present," Ingersoll said.

Jesse didn't answer.

"What have you told him?" Ingersoll said to his wife.

"What is there to tell, Jay?" she said.

"This is harassment," Ingersoll said to Jesse.

Jesse smiled and didn't say anything.

"And you know it is," Ingersoll said. "Don't you."

Jesse smiled some more.

"Can't you make him leave me alone?" Betsy Ingersoll said.

"I can," Ingersoll said, "and I will."

"I wish you would," Betsy said. "In fact, Jay, I wish you already had."

"I told you," Ingersoll said, "if he approached you in any way you were to call me at once."

"Yes," she said. "You did."

"But you chose to disobey me," Ingersoll said.

"I know," she said.

"We'll discuss that later," Ingersoll said.

"Why later?" she said.

Ingersoll shook his head.

"Stone," he said, "I have spoken to the district attorney about you."

"He mentioned that," Jesse said.

"And I have spoken to your board of selectmen," Ingersoll said. "You will, I'm sure, hear from them shortly."

"Doubtless," Jesse said.

"Why not now," Betsy Ingersoll said.

"What?" Ingersoll said.

"Why can't we discuss my disobedience right now," she said.

"For God's sake, Betsy. We're in the police chief's office."

"Perfect," she said. "You can have him arrest me for disobedience."

Jesse could see Ingersoll fighting his temper.

"I have no plans for that, Betsy."

Ingersoll smiled.

"Let's pursue it at home," he said.

"When will that be?" she said.

"When will we be home?" Ingersoll said.

"I'll be home pretty soon," Betsy said. "But you. When will you be home?"

"When you are," Ingersoll said.

Puzzlement was pressing for position with anger in his response.

"That will be refreshing," she said.

Puzzlement was winning.

"That I'm home?" he said.

"You so rarely are," Betsy said.

Ingersoll looked as if he'd been physically jostled. He stared at her.

"Betsy," he said finally, "I am the managing partner of the biggest law firm north of New York. I work long hours, and I work very hard."

"I know how hard you're working," she said. "And at what."

Ingersoll said to Jesse, "Could you excuse us for a moment?"

"You mean step out of my office?" Jesse said.

"Yes."

"No," Jesse said. "You're free to leave."

Ingersoll stood silently.

The he said, "Betsy. Time to go."

"You go along, Jay," she said. "I'm not through here."

He stood silent again.

Then he said to her, "God, you're an embarrassment," and turned and left the office.

Jesse looked at Betsy and waited.

"He orders me around like I'm some kind of junior law clerk," she said.

Jesse nodded.

"I'm his wife, for God's sake," she said.

Jesse nodded again.

"He ought to pay more attention to that," she said.

Jesse waited. Betsy Ingersoll didn't say any more.

"Is it that he orders you around?" Jesse said.

"It's a lot of things," Betsy said. "Are we through here?"

"I think we probably are," Jesse said. "For the moment."

# 26

"Have you seen me?" Jenn said when Jesse answered the phone.

"On the tube?" Jesse said.

"Yes, silly, where else?"

Jesse sipped his first drink of the night, carefully, so Jenn wouldn't hear.

"I haven't," Jesse said.

"Probably not syndicated up there yet. But we will be. The show is really taking off."

"I'll keep an eye out," Jesse said.

"I've been doing a style report every Wednesday morning and some interviews, and of course the weather."

"For the whole syndication area?" Jesse said.

"You know," Jenn said, "one of those generic reports: *Weather in the east is mostly clear and mild. There are some storm clouds in the area of Chesapeake Bay, and unseasonable temperatures along the coast of Maine. Now, here's the forecast for your area.* Cut to local news, one minute."

"Find a place to live?" Jesse said.

"Downtown," Jenn said. "Nice little studio on Tenth Street, between Fifth and Sixth. Rent-controlled."

"Sublet?" Jesse said.

"No, my friend has had it since rent control," Jenn said.

"You sublet from your friend?"

"No, we share," Jenn said.

"Helps with the rent," Jesse said.

He took another drink, carefully.

"Yes," Jenn said.

Jesse didn't say anything.

"Well, actually," Jenn said, "I guess he pays the rent."

Jesse finished his drink.

"Helps quite a bit with the rent," Jesse said.

Jesse considered whether he could make another drink without Jenn's knowing.

"I'm trying to be honest with you, Jesse," she said. "Please don't make it harder for me."

"Sure," Jesse said.

"We've always been honest with each other," Jenn said.

"Actually," Jesse said, "we haven't."

"Well, it's not too late to start," Jenn said.

"Nope," Jesse said.

He stood and walked to the bar, took a handful of ice from the bucket, and put it in his glass.

"Are you drinking?" Jenn said.

"You bet," Jesse said.

He broke the phone connection and shut off the answering machine. Then he put more ice in the glass, added some scotch to his usual level, and filled the glass with soda. The phone didn't ring again. He took a long pull on the drink and sat on a bar stool and looked at Ozzie's picture. He nodded to himself. He could never have been Ozzie, but he could have made the show. Whenever he looked at Ozzie's picture he remembered. Playing at Pueblo.

The three-hopper to the right side. The runner coming down from first. The second baseman's feed, a little high, as Jesse covered second. The takeout slide was a clean one, but it caught him as he was reaching for the throw and trying to stay with the bag. He flipped. He landed on his right shoulder. He hung on to the ball, but they missed the double play, and his shoulder was broken. It was his last professional game. He stood and walked to his French doors and stared out at the harbor. He had no claim on Jenn. They were divorced. He slept with other women. She slept with other men. She started it. They were still married when she started it. Jesse took in more scotch. That was then. This is now. It all seemed a downward spiral. He was going to be a big-league shortstop, and then he wasn't. He was a detective in Robbery Homicide in Los Angeles. Then he wasn't. He was married to Jenn. Then he wasn't. He finished his drink and went back to the bar and made another one. He gestured with the full glass at the picture.

"You and me, Wizard," he said.

Now he was a small-town cop in the far corner of the country, drinking alone at night and talking to a fucking baseball poster. He took his glass to his chair and sat and looked at the phone. No need to turn the answering machine off, she wasn't calling back anyway. He reached over and turned it on. He looked around the empty room and took a drink.

"After this, what?" he said aloud in the empty room.

He sat and thought about what he'd said, and nodded his head slowly, and smiled faintly to himself.

"Nothing," he said. "Nothing at all."

# 27

Molly had patched the desk phone into the conference room, and everyone but Arthur Angstrom and Buddy Hall was in there.

"We've had two more home invasions," Jesse said. "Three so far. Pretty much the same M.O. Women home alone in the daytime. Man comes in with a mask and a gun, forces them to disrobe, takes their picture, makes them lie facedown and count to a hundred, and disappears."

"He dress the same?" Suit said.

"Black pants, black windbreaker," Jesse said. "Ski mask. Baseball hat, probably Yankees. The women aren't sure."

"Nobody in the neighborhood noticed anything?" Maguire said.

"Nope," Jesse said. "Not that many people around. Most people's husbands and wives both work. Kids are in school."

"Do we know if he was in a car or on foot?" Suit said.

"Nope."

"He dresses like our peeper," Molly said. "Think it might be him."

"They don't usually escalate like that," Suit said.

Jesse looked at him.

"I been reading up," Suit said.

He had a yellow legal pad on the table in front of him, and a ballpoint pen. Jesse nodded and went to the big pot on the file cabinet and got some coffee. There was a box of doughnuts on the table. He took one.

"Any thoughts?" he said.

He took a bite of the doughnut, leaning forward so he wouldn't get cinnamon sugar on his shirt front.

"We see a pattern anywhere?" Suit said.

"The women," Molly said. "All of them in their forties. All of them married, with children in school."

"All of them in neighborhoods which are relatively deserted during the day," Suit said. "At least the school day."

"So, which is the appeal?" Jesse said. "Married? Children? Forty?"

"Alone during the day?" Maguire said.

"Relatively upscale neighborhoods," Suit said.

"All of the above?" Molly said.

"Age is maybe a function of other things," Molly said. "Most women with kids in school would be in their thirties or forties."

"Like you, Moll," Suit said.

"Like hell," Molly said. "I'm the same age as my oldest kid."

"How's that work?" Suit said.

"It just does," Molly said.

Jesse looked at Maguire.

"Any reports of our Peeping Tom since the first home invasion?" Jesse said.

"No," Maguire said.

"We have to consider that it may be the same guy," Jesse said.

"We don't know who he is," Suit said. "So what we consider don't make a hell of a lot of difference."

Jesse ignored him.

"And we can also entertain the possibility that it's not," Jesse said.

"The peeper was my case, Jesse," Maguire said. "Are the home invasions mine, too?"

"The home-invasions case belongs to all of us," Jesse said. "If it is our peeper, he's escalating, and we have no way to know how far it'll go."

No one said anything.

"Molly and I will keep talking to the victims," Jesse said. "I want each of you to listen to everybody you know, questions, gossip, idle chitchat, thoughtful discussion, jokes, whatever, and always listening for anything that might send you somewhere, tell you something, lead you anywhere."

No one said anything.

"A good police force," Jesse said, "allows people to feel safe in their homes."

Everyone was quiet.

"We need to do better," Jesse said

No one spoke. Everyone looked glum.

Jesse grinned.

"Win one for the Stoner?" he said.

They all looked relieved.

"Okay," Jesse said. "Time to go back to work. Molly, you fill in Arthur and Buddy.

Suit, stick around for a minute. Everybody else . . ." He jerked his thumb toward the door and they got up and left. Suit stayed sitting at the table with his yellow pad.

"We get all the rest of the doughnuts," he said.

He reached into the box and took one.

"You still talking to the swingers?" Jesse said.

"Sure," Suit said. "Can't say I'm learning much."

"See if they have anyone in their group that especially likes to watch."

Suit nodded as he chewed down half a doughnut.

When it was swallowed he said, "You think it might be one of the swingers?"

"No," Jesse said. "To tell you the truth, I don't. But I got nowhere else to go, and at least the swingers group is atypical in their sexuality."

"It'll take a while," Suit said. "I have to do a lot of schmoozing to get a little information, you know?"

"It's called police work," Jesse said.

"Awful long shot," Suit said.

"At the moment, I don't have a shorter one," Jesse said.

Suit nodded. He finished his doughnut.

"You think this guy will do something worse?"

"If he's our peeper, he went up the ladder pretty quick," Jesse said.

"They dress the same," Suit said.

"Could be a copycat," Jesse said. "Could be on purpose to mislead us."

"Or it could be him," Suit said.

"Or it could be him," Jesse said.

"I'll see what I can find out," Suit said.

# 28

"So," Spike said, "you two got anything going these days?"

"What we've got going," Sunny said, "as you well know, is my ex-husband, and Jesse's ex-wife."

"It's a start," Spike said.

Jesse smiled.

"How are things with Marcy Campbell?" Jesse said.

The three of them were sitting on the deck of the Gray Gull as the sun set behind them, stretching the shadows of the boats at mooring toward Paradise Neck.

"Good," Spike said. "She really likes you."

"Everybody does," Jesse said. "Is she finding you any property?"

"She doesn't do commercial real estate, but she is co-brokering with a guy who does."

"Find anything?" Jesse said.

He was drinking beer. Spike had a Maker's Mark on the rocks. Sunny sipped some Riesling.

"Yep," Spike said.

"You did?" Sunny said.

"Yep."

"Well, where?" Sunny said.

Spike grinned.

"Right here," he said.

"The Gray Gull?" Sunny said.

"Yep, soon to be Spike's North."

"My God," Sunny said.

"Congratulations," Jesse said.

"But you can't call it Spike's North," Sunny said.

"Why not?"

"Because it's the Gray Gull," Sunny said. "It's been here forever."

"Or at least since you started fooling around with the chief," Spike said.

"At least that long," Sunny said. "The name's got history. People will be mad if you change it."

"Like I should care," Spike said.

"Customers will be mad at you," Sunny said.

Spike smiled at Sunny. She often referred to Spike as her "compliance consultant," and Jesse could see why. He wasn't unusually tall. But he had about him the massive shapeless force of a bear.

"Like, I do care," he said. "How about Spike's Gray Gull?"

"Ick," Sunny said.

"Okay," Spike said. "Gray Gull."

"A proven winner," Sunny said

"Sound right to you, Chief Jesse?" Spike said.

Spike's receding hair was cut very close to his skull and his beard was trimmed short. There was a shiny go-to-hell look in his eyes.

"'Fooling around'?" Jesse said.

"Fooling around what?" Spike said.

"Sunny and I weren't fooling around," Jesse said. "We were serious."

"Ah," Spike said. "Excellent. If I weren't

gayer than laughter, I'd be serious about her, too."

"Would you like to talk about me further?" Sunny said. "I'll try to be quiet."

"When I heard you were a private dick, I was hopeful," Spike said. "But then when I met you my hopes were dashed."

"Short for detective," Sunny said.

"Sure," Spike said. "Now you tell me."

Sunny giggled.

"When do you close?" Jesse said.

"Sixty days," Spike said. "Then if you want, you can run a tab here."

"What I need," Jesse said. "An open tab at a bar."

# 29

Jesse sat in his office, reading a letter from the Night Hawk.

**Dear Chief Stone,**

**I know you have been looking for me. I am your Peeping Tom, and I am the one who forced those women to undress so I could take their pictures (see enclosed, so you know it's really me). When I'm doing that, I am in some sort of feverish coma. When it's over I feel disgusted with myself and swear that I'll never do it again. But I do. I am really afraid I might do something**

even worse than what I'm doing. When I'm in the coma, I seem to be somebody else. I guess it's some kind of obsession. The funny thing about it is how I get pleasure from it when I do it, but overall it's ruining my life. Maybe it's the nature of obsessions. I hate it. I hate myself. I've seen plenty of naked women in my life. But never enough for my obsession. I won't turn myself in. I probably should, but my obsession won't let me. I guess I can't. And I don't even know if this letter is a cri de coeur asking for help, or if it's part of my obsession to taunt you. What I know is that my life is becoming more unbearable every time I act out my obsession. . . . But I need to see, I need to know their secret.

**The Night Hawk**

Jesse picked up the three pictures that had come with the letter. They were remarkably similar. A frightened and humiliated woman standing naked, looking into the camera. The women even looked somewhat alike. Dark hair, not fat, about the same height. What secret were they revealing? Their naked selves? You could go online and find thousands of pictures of nude women. What was special about these women? Maybe it wasn't about nudity or sex. Maybe it was about control, about power. In most men, Jesse suspected, sex and power were not unrelated. Did it matter that they looked superficially alike? Most women of their age and weight and social status would probably look pretty much like they did, if forced to stand naked in front of a stranger's camera. Why had he written? Was it that he wanted to get caught? Or was he like those people who had sex in public places, the experience intensified by the possibility of getting caught? Or both.

Jesse took the pictures to his office window and looked at them carefully in the sunlight. They told him nothing. The Night Hawk had obviously used a digital camera and fed the pictures into his computer, and printed them out on ordinary printer paper. He turned the pictures over. Nothing. He turned them back faceup. Nothing. Nothing to tell him what computer, or what printer, or even what kind of camera. He went back to his desk and took a lavender file folder from a desk drawer. Molly bought his office supplies, and she liked colorful file folders. He spread the three pictures out on his desktop and covered them one at a time with the file folder and then slid the folder down an inch at a time, looking at each narrow segment of the picture as the folder revealed it. Nothing. He did the same with the letter. Nothing. He took the letter to the window and studied it in the sunlight. Ordinary paper. Common typeface. He went back to his desk and put the three photographs in the lavender folder with the letter on top of them. Then he went to his office door and yelled for Molly.

"Close the door," he said when she came in.

She did, and sat down in front of his desk. Jesse handed her the folder.

"Read the letter first," Jesse said. "Then look at the pictures."

Molly nodded and opened the folder. She read the letter and looked at the pictures, and when she was done she put everything back in the folder, closed the folder, and put it on the edge of Jesse's desk.

"The son of a bitch," she said.

Jesse nodded.

"You've been over these?"

"From every angle I could think of," Jesse said.

"Prints?"

"Not yet," Jesse said. "You can have Peter Perkins go over them, in your presence."

"In my presence?"

"I want you to take care of these pictures," Jesse said. "I give them to anybody else in the department and they'll be in the copy machine thirty seconds later."

"What is it with men and nudity," Molly said.

"I guess we're in favor of it," Jesse said.

"I mean, I've been married seventeen years," Molly said. "My husband has seen me naked maybe five thousand times. But every time I come out of the shower or whatever he looks at me like he's peeking in a window."

Jesse nodded.

"What's that about?" Molly said.

"I don't know," Jesse said.

"Are you like that?" Molly said.

Jesse nodded slowly.

"Pretty much," he said.

"In the time you've been a cop," Molly said, "have you ever heard of a female Peeping Tom?"

"Nope."

"I don't get it," Molly said.

"Me either."

"I mean, have no interest in seeing a man with his clothes off," Molly said.

"Not even certain Native Americans from the Apache tribe?" Jesse said.

"Oh, hell," Molly said. "Will you ever let up on that?"

"I have no plans to," Jesse said.

"One little indiscretion," she said. "Why did I ever tell you?"

"I'm the chief of police," Jesse said.

Molly nodded.

"Sad but true," she said. "So, is this part of my case?"

"We gotta hang on to the pictures," Jesse said. "They're evidence. But I don't want a bunch of male cops looking at nude pictures of them. I don't want those women humiliated any more than they have been."

Molly nodded again and picked up the folder. She stood for a moment, looking at Jesse.

"You're not so bad," she said. "For a guy."

"If only I were Apache," Jesse said.

Molly looked at him for another moment.

"Oh, fuck you," she said.

"Hey," Jesse said. "How 'bout a little respect."

Molly grinned.

"Oh, fuck you, Chief," she said, and left the office.

# 30

Jesse brought a copy of the Night Hawk's letter with him when he went to see Dix.

"Could you read this for me?" Jesse said.

Dix nodded and picked up the letter. He read it carefully and handed it back to Jesse.

"The serial home invader in Paradise?" Dix said.

"Yes. There were pictures of his victims, but I didn't bring them."

"No need," Dix said.

"Whaddya think?" Jesse said.

Dix tipped his chair back with his elbows resting on the arms and his fingers laced across his flat stomach.

"He seems to understand himself," Dix said.

"You don't think he's crazy?" Jesse said.

"I do," Dix said. "And that is what he seems to understand."

Jesse nodded.

"Anything in there that will help me catch him?"

"Not much," Dix said. "Tell me about the women."

"Married, mothers, all around forty, dark hair, good-enough-looking, but not head-turners."

"Three so far," Dix said.

"Yes."

"So we may have some idea of what kind of woman he favors."

"Kind of a small sample," Jesse said.

"It's all you have at the moment," Dix said. "Theory of the case?"

"Guy likes to take pictures of naked women," Jesse said.

Dix smiled.

"Hard to argue against that," he said.

"Anything you see in the letter?" Jesse said. "Besides he knows he's crazy?"

"He promises to keep doing it," Dix said.

"It's my impression that it is unusual for Peeping Toms to graduate to home invasion," Jesse said.

"That is my impression as well," Dix said.

"But it happens."

"Yes," Dix said.

"And it happened with this guy," Jesse said.

"Unless he's lying about being the Peeping Tom."

"You think he is?"

"Don't know," Dix said.

"So, say it's the truth. Why would someone take that step?"

"There's no way to know, as was the case with your panty checker," Dix said. "We have no idea what all of this means to him."

"Peeping Tom work is so much less dangerous," Jesse said. "And if you are caught, the consequences are much less severe."

"Maybe that's the charm of home invasion," Dix said.

"The risk?"

"It seems from his letter that he wants to be caught," Dix said.

"So we just sit around and wait until he catches himself?" Jesse said.

"He also doesn't want to be caught," Dix said.

"Conflicted," Jesse said.

Dix smiled and nodded.

"And obsessive," Jesse said.

Dix smiled and nodded again.

"If we knew why," Jesse said.

"Probably wouldn't do you much good," Dix said. "A lot of obsessions are rooted in long-ago events that the obsessed aren't even aware of."

Jesse nodded.

"I mean, pretty much every guy I know would look at a nude woman if he could," Jesse said.

Dix nodded.

"Wouldn't you?"

Dix smiled.

"I'm behind the desk," Dix said. "You're in front of it."

"Which means I don't get to know any-thing about you?" Jesse said.

"You know several things," Dix said.

"I know you used to be a cop and you used to be a drunk," Jesse said.

"And you also know that I have a Ph.D. from Chicago, and an M.D. from Harvard."

"How would I know that?" Jesse said.

"And you a trained detective," Dix said.

He pointed to the diplomas framed on his wall.

"Okay," Jesse said. "But you know what I'm saying. Most men are interested in female nudity."

"Most straight men," Dix said.

Jesse nodded.

"But most men don't do what this guy does," he said.

"Because they are not driven by his need," Dix said.

"So what the fuck is his need?" Jesse said.

"There may be a clue," Dix said. "In the letter he speaks of a need to see."

"'I need to see,'" Jesse quoted. "'I need to know their secret.'"

"You didn't miss it," Dix said.

"What's the secret?" Jesse said.

"We have no way to know," Dix said.

"How about a guess?" Jesse said. "Anything is better than nothing."

Dix paused and didn't speak for a moment.

"There was a famous British aesthete," Dix said, "who, on his wedding night, was so traumatized by the sight of his bride's pubic hair that he could not consummate the marriage."

"He was a virgin?" Jesse said.

"Apparently," Dix said.

"That had to be a while ago," Jesse said.

"Long time, yes," Dix said. "It is difficult, in our time, to reach marriage age without being aware that women have pubic hair."

"But," Jesse said. "If it was a kid discovering that . . ."

"And the circumstances were sufficiently traumatizing . . ." Dix said.

"The shameful secret," Jesse said.

Dix nodded.

"Every woman's shameful secret," Jesse said.

"To one degree or another," Dix said.

"He might need to keep going over it," Jesse said.

Dix shrugged.

"Might," he said.

"Either because he is hoping it won't be true this time?" Jesse said.

"Or because he wants to reaffirm the essential baseness of women," Dix said.

"And the pictures would be evidence," Jesse said. "Proof of the secret."

"Maybe," Dix said. "You've interviewed the victims?"

"Of course."

"Did he touch them?"

"No. He never got close to them," Jesse said.

"Threaten them?"

"Just along the lines of 'Do what I say and you won't get hurt,'" Jesse said.

"Verbally abusive?"

"No," Jesse said. "Course, it might not be that."

"True," Dix said.

"Might be something entirely different," Jesse said.

"Might," Dix said.

"So what difference does it make?" Jesse said.

"None that I can see," Dix said.

"So why are we talking about it?"

"It's your session," Dix said.

Jesse was silent for a moment.

Then he said, "Maybe it's better than talking about me."

Dix nodded and looked at his watch.

"Or maybe you think it is," Dix said. "Let's talk about that next time."

# 31

Suit came into Jesse's office and sat down across the desk from him.

"And now," he said, "this update from swingers' correspondent Suitcase Simpson."

"You converted yet?"

"I been trying to," Suit said. "But like I told you, no single guys."

"Maybe you could bring Cissy Hathaway," Jesse said.

"That's over," Suit said. "She's too old for me."

"Lotta people are," Jesse said. "Whaddya got?"

"I been talking to Kim Magruder—Kim Clark—like you said."

"And?"

Suit shrugged.

"I feel kind of bad for her," Suit said. "I mean, she was the golden girl, you know, going steady with the star quarterback."

"Chase Clark," Jesse said.

"Yeah, and he knocked her up. And she was real Catholic and"—Suit shrugged—"they had to get married."

"And produced Missy," Jesse said.

"Yep. They got a little boy, too. Eric."

"Why do you feel sorry for her?" Jesse said.

"One, because she's married to Chase Clark, who's a fucking jerk. Two, because she doesn't like the swinging thing. But does it because she thinks she has to, to save her marriage."

"She say so?"

"Not exactly. But I'm pretty sure," Suit said.

Jesse nodded.

"She more talkative about things this time?"

"Yeah, much," Suit said. "Once we were

alone, you know, Debbie Lupo wasn't around."

"Now Debbie Basco," Jesse said.

"Right," Suit said. "Once Debbie wasn't around, Kimmy kind of relaxed. We talked a little about high school and me dating her kid sister and where Tammy is now, and what she's doing, and like that. But from the start it seemed like she wanted to talk about the wife-swapping thing. Like she needed to talk with someone about it."

Jesse nodded again.

"She's known you since you were kids. You used to date her little sister."

"It was like, how threatening could I be?" Suit said. "Little Luther Simpson."

"She calls you Luther?"

"Never mind about that," Suit said.

"Anything that might help us with the Night Hawk?" Jesse said.

"I'm not sure," Suit said. "There are people who like to watch their spouse with someone else."

"Men?" Jesse said.

"Yeah."

"Names?"

"She won't tell me names," Suit said. "It's like a club rule."

"You think if you brought her in, she'd talk to me?" Jesse said.

"Not here," Suit said.

"Where?" Jesse said.

"I don't know," Suit said. "I'll ask her. What do I tell her about why?"

"I got two reasons," Jesse said. "One is the Night Hawk, and two is her daughter."

"I thought you promised the daughter you wouldn't give her away."

"I did, and I won't. It's why I need to talk with her," Jesse said. "I have to feel my way along."

"I can't tell her that," Suit said.

"I know," Jesse said. "I'll meet her anywhere she wants."

"So what do I tell her it's for."

"You'll think of something," Jesse said.

# 32

"This is on me," Marcy Campbell said to Jesse. "For the business you sent me."

They sat across from each other at a window table in the Gray Gull.

"I thought you were doing me a favor," Jesse said.

"Nope. I got to co-broker with Chuck Derby and get half his commission for very little work."

"Well, good for me," Jesse said. "I accept."

"I knew you would," Marcy said.

She was a handsome woman, several

years older than Jesse, divorced, with grown children.

"Spike seems an unusual man," Marcy said.

"I believe he is," Jesse said. "But he's Sunny Randall's best friend."

"And you like Sunny a lot," Marcy said.

"I do."

The waitress brought a vodka gimlet for Marcy, scotch and soda for Jesse.

"But not as much as Jenn," Marcy said.

Jesse looked into his glass for a moment.

"I don't know," Jesse said.

"You don't?"

"I don't."

"My God," Marcy said.

Jesse shrugged.

"I'm trying to rethink things," Jesse said.

"She's gone again?" Marcy said.

"She's in New York," Jesse said.

"Alone?" Marcy said.

"Not likely," Jesse said.

Marcy nodded.

"Good news and bad," Marcy said.

"The good news?"

"That you're starting to rethink."

"You've never been a fan of Jenn's," Jesse said.

"I've always been a fan of yours," Marcy said.

"And you've said your say already about Jenn."

"Yes," Marcy said.

"No need to plow that field again," Jesse said.

"No," Marcy said.

They each drank a little.

"Too bad we don't want to get married," Jesse said. "We get along so well."

"Maybe if we wanted to get married," Marcy said, "we wouldn't get along so well."

"Possible," Jesse said.

He drank some more scotch.

"You've slept with a lot of men," Jesse said.

"Excuse me?" Marcy said.

"Oh, stop it," Jesse said. "We've both slept with a lot of people, and enjoyed it, and neither one of us is embarrassed about it."

"Well," Marcy said. "Yes."

"Any of the men you know that didn't want to look at you naked?"

"Didn't?" Marcy said.

"Didn't," Jesse said.

"Are you implying something dreadful about my body?" Marcy said.

"No," Jesse said. "I'm serious. Do you know any straight men who don't want to look at a woman naked?"

"No," Marcy said.

"Do you want to look at men with their clothes off?"

"What kind of survey is this?" Marcy said.

"Bear with me," Jesse said. "Does male nudity interest you?"

"If a man's in good shape, and we're in the process of making love, yes, I sort of like to look at his body."

"If I had a bunch of pictures of naked men, would you want to look?"

"No."

"What about male strippers?" Jesse said. "Many women seem interested in them."

"I'm not," Marcy said. "I think that's mostly about proving what wild-and-crazy girls they are."

"You know any pornography for women?"

"Not for straight women," Marcy said.

"Whorehouses for women?"

"Where women go to have sex with male prostitutes?" Marcy said.

"Yeah."

"Ugh," Marcy said.

"I'll take that as a no."

Jesse finished his drink and looked around for the waitress.

"This is about that guy that breaks in and photographs women," Marcy said.

"I guess," Jesse said.

"You're trying to figure him out," Marcy said.

"I guess."

"Jesse," she said. "Maybe there's a difference between normal male impulse and this guy."

Jesse nodded.

"He doesn't forcibly photograph nude women because he's a man," Marcy said. "He does it because he's a wack job."

The waitress came with their next round.

"So I don't have to wrestle with gender guilt," Jesse said.

"You have enough to wrestle with," Marcy said, "without worrying about basic differences between the sexes."

Jesse raised his glass.

*"Vive la différence,"* he said.

Marcy smiled.

"I'll drink to that," she said.

They looked at their menus quietly for a time.

"What's bothersome," Jesse said, "is that even in normal men, whatever that quite means, there's never enough."

"You mean no matter how many women you see naked, you want to see another one?" Marcy said.

"Or the same one again."

"That's probably why he takes the pictures," Marcy said.

"Maybe," Jesse said. "It also suggests that he'll keep going."

"And that's what you're worried about," Marcy said.

"Yep."

"It is sort of crazy, isn't it," Marcy said. "Lot of men like to take pictures of wives and girlfriends."

"Whom they've often seen naked," Jesse said.

"And will again."

"Maybe it's not exactly about the nudity," Jesse said.

"Even if it isn't," Marcy said, "how does that help you?"

"I don't know," Jesse said. "I just figure the more I understand about him, the better chance I have to get him."

"It would probably be even more helpful if you knew what, exactly, it *is* about," Marcy said.

"Sooner or later," Jesse said.

"You really believe that?"

"Have to," Jesse said, "to keep being a cop. I know better, but I still have to believe that if I keep looking at it and turning it around and rolling around on it, eventually I'll come up with something."

"To be the kind of cop you are," Marcy said.

Jesse shrugged.

"Anybody take pictures of you?"

"Sure," Marcy said.

Jesse smiled.

"Got any on you?" he said.

"No," Marcy said. "But perhaps later this evening there'll be a photo op."

"I was hopeful," Jesse said.

# 33

Suit brought Kimberly Clark into Jesse's office.

"Kim Clark," he said. "Jesse Stone."

They said hello and Kim Clark sat in a chair in front of Jesse's desk. Suit looked at Jesse.

"On your way out," Jesse said to him, "ask Molly to step in."

Suit nodded and left. Kim Clark looked after him. Molly came in.

"Molly Crane," Jesse said. "Kim Clark."

They said hello. Kim was a smallish woman, neat figure, too much dark hair, about forty. Jesse could see her daughter in her.

"I saw both of you at the school," Kim Clark said. "That business with Mrs. Ingersoll."

Jesse nodded.

"I've asked Molly to join us, as I do whenever I'm talking with a woman in my office," Jesse said. "Unless you object."

"I have no objection," Kim Clark said.

"This is a first-name police department," Jesse said. "I'm Jesse. She's Molly, and I hope we may call you Kim."

"Of course," Kim said. "Why am I here?"

"As I'm sure Suit explained," Jesse said, "we're investigating a case unrelated to you, but we feel that you might be able to help us."

"I'm not in trouble, am I?" Kim said. "Luther said I wasn't in trouble."

"No, no," Jesse said. "Of course not. I'm just hoping you can give us some information that will help us."

"Is it about the swinging?"

"You are not in trouble," Jesse said. "About the swinging or anything else. But I am looking for information about swinging."

"It's perfectly legal," she said.

"I know," Jesse said.

"I've always been sort of fascinated with it, to tell you the truth," Molly said. "We haven't actually done anything yet, but my husband and I have certainly discussed it."

"It's very freeing," Kim said.

"I can see how it would be," Molly said.

"Did you know that the incidence of divorce is lower among swingers?" Kim said.

"I didn't know that," Jesse said.

"And infidelity," Kim said.

"Of course," Jesse said. "Everything is right out in the open."

Kim nodded.

"I don't mean to be nosy," Molly said. "But is it really?"

"Is it really what?" Kim said.

"Right out in the open?"

"You mean the, ah . . ."

"The sex," Molly said. "I mean, do you get to watch each other?"

"If you wish," Kim said.

"Wow," Molly said. "That sounds like it would be fun. Do you and your husband see each other?"

"Sometimes," Kim said.

Her face was flushed. She didn't look at Jesse.

"Wow," Jesse said. "I'm not so sure I could perform. Is it possible to just watch?"

"Some people do that," Kim said.

"Men and women?"

"Men mostly," Kim said.

"Is there anyone who just watches?" Jesse said.

"I don't know," Kim said.

"Anyone come alone?"

"No," Kim said. "No single men."

"Single women?"

"I don't think it's against the rules, but women aren't into it that much."

"Really?" Molly said. "I thought it sounded exciting."

Kim's mouth clamped shut for a moment before she spoke.

"Not to anyone I know," Kim said.

Molly smiled and shrugged.

"Well, it's all about freedom," Molly said. "Isn't it?"

Kim nodded.

"Who's the biggest watcher?" Jesse said.

"Oh, I can't tell you anyone's name," Kim said.

"Kim," Jesse said. "We've staked out your house. You had what appeared to be a party there three weeks ago. We have photos of who came and went. We have the plate numbers of all the cars. We've checked the registrations. We know who's in the club. We only want you to tell us which ones like best to watch."

"You . . . you can't do that," Kim said. "We're within our rights."

"We can do it. We did do it, and yes, you're within your rights," Jesse said. "But I need to know who likes to watch. And I can question everyone in your club until I find out, but it would be easier if you told me now."

"That's not true," she said. "You're just saying that."

Jesse nodded and opened his middle drawer. He took out a sheet of paper and began to read.

"Mr. and Mrs. Martin Felts, Ralph Alfonzo and Maria Dupree, Mr. and Mrs. Clyde Crosland . . ."

"Oh, God," Kim said.

"Shall I go on?" Jesse said.

"No," Kim said. "No."

Jesse nodded and put the paper back in his middle drawer.

"How did you find out in the first place?" Kim said.

Jesse shook his head.

"Doesn't matter," he said.

"But they'll know you got their names by watching my house," Kim said.

"Yes," Jesse said.

"And you'd question my husband."

"Yes."

"So he'd know," Kim said.

Jesse waited. Kim's eyes began to fill.

"Why can't you just leave us alone?" Kim said. "We're not harming anyone."

"Just looking for a name," Jesse said.

Kim looked at Molly. Molly smiled encouragingly. Kim looked back at Jesse, and quickly around the small room.

Then she said, "Seth."

"Seth?"

"Seth Ralston," she said.

"He ever watch you?" Jesse said.

Kim's face reddened again.

"Yes."

"Others?"

"We all talk about how he mostly doesn't want to actually do it."

"We?"

"All the girls," Kim said.

"So what does his partner do while he's watching?" Molly said.

Kim shrugged.

"Sometimes she does a three-way with Hannah and Hannah's partner."

"Hannah is?" Jesse said.

"Seth's wife," Kim said. "Hannah Wechsler."

Jesse nodded.

"Thanks, Kim," he said. "That's a great help. Do you need a ride home?"

"No," she said. "I have my car."

Jesse stood and put his hand out. Kim shook it. Molly stood, too.

"I won't have to come again, will I?" Kim said.

"Oh," Jesse said. "No. Of course not."

# 34

"You mean that?" Molly said.

"What?"

"That she won't have to come in again?"

"No," Jesse said. "I didn't. I just figured we'd squeezed her enough for today."

"Yes," Molly said. "She was going to break down on us if we pushed her more."

"I still have the issue of the kid to deal with."

"We skirted around that pretty good," Molly said.

"We did," Jesse said.

"Course, Kim's not the brightest bulb in the string," Molly said.

"You think she likes swinging?" Jesse said.

"No."

"So why do you think she does it?" Jesse said

"I don't know, but I'll guess it has to do with her husband."

"I was starting to worry about you," Jesse said.

"I was pretty convincing," Molly said.

Jesse grinned.

"When you decide to get into swinging," he said, "can I watch?"

"Ugh!" Molly said.

"'Ugh' about swinging, or 'ugh' about me watching."

"All of the above," Molly said. "I especially like her saying that there's less infidelity among swingers."

"Depends on how you define 'unfaithful,'" Jesse said.

"Like it's okay if we both do it?" Molly said.

"Or it's okay if we each give permission to the other one," Jesse said.

"Right," Molly said. "Eat this apple, Adam. It's okay if we both take a bite."

"Boy, are you retro," Jesse said.

"I am," Molly said. "And no remarks about Native Americans."

*"Moi?"* Jesse said.

*"Vous,"* Molly said. "My one-night stand with Crow was infidelity. I'm not exactly sorry I did it. But it was unfaithful to my husband and my marriage, and I know it and don't pretend otherwise."

"You love your husband," Jesse said.

"I do, and did while I was unfaithful."

"You're okay with it?"

"Yes."

"What if he'd given permission?"

"Permission, shmission," Molly said. "It's still infidelity, and gussying it up with a bunch of free-to-be-you-and-me crap doesn't make it otherwise."

"So you were just pretending when you told her how tempting it was to you," Jesse said.

"I was," Molly said.

"God, you were good," Jesse said.

"Everybody says that," Molly said.

Jesse grinned again.

"Does this mean I'm not going to get the chance to watch," he said.

"I'll put you on the list," Molly said. "We gonna look into Mr. Ralston?"

"We are," Jesse said. "Ms. Wechsler, too, I think."

"How about the Clark kids?" Molly said.

"Step at a time," Jesse said. "First I'll find the Night Hawk, then we'll save the children."

"And after that?" Molly said.

"Probably leap a tall building," Jesse said. "At a single bound."

# 35

"I simply couldn't do it," Gloria Fisher said. "I simply would not."

Jesse sat across from her in her living room. Molly sat beside her on the couch.

"Tell me about it," Jesse said. "From the beginning."

Gloria nodded. She was like the others, dark-haired, trim, in her early forties.

"My husband went to work. I got my daughter off to school, took a shower, got dressed, and when I came out of the bedroom, he was here."

"Door unlocked?" Jesse said.

"I guess it was. It's stupid. I knew this

had been happening. But I forgot. . . ." She spread her hands. "I'm terrible about locking up. Anyway, I said, 'What the fuck do you want?' And he pointed his gun at me and said, 'Do what I say and I won't hurt you.' And I was enraged. . . . I said, 'Like hell.' And he said, 'Take off your clothes,' and I said, 'Like hell.' It's funny, I wasn't scared, I was very, very angry. The sonovabitch came in my house. . . . Now I'm scared."

Molly nodded.

"That's because now it's safe to be scared."

"I guess," Gloria said.

"So what did he do?" Jesse said.

He said, 'Undress or I'll shoot you.' And I said, 'Get out of my fucking house.' And his eyes got really big and he took a step toward me and then stopped, and, like, stared at me, and then he turned around and ran out of the house."

"Did you see his car?"

"No."

"Which way he went?"

"No," Gloria said. "I went right to the phone and called nine-one-one and Officer Friedman was here in like a minute."

Jesse looked at Steve Friedman, standing in the kitchen door.

"I was two blocks away," Steve said. "I didn't see him."

"Description?"

"Oh, about my husband's size, I would say. Five-eleven, hundred and eighty-five pounds. Black jacket and pants, black ski mask, had on those latex gloves like doctors use."

"The gun?"

"I don't know anything about guns," she said. "It looked small to me, kind of silver-colored."

Jesse nodded.

"Any sign of a camera?"

"I think so," Gloria said. "I think he had some sort of digital camera in his other hand."

"Which hand had the gun?" Jesse said.

Gloria closed her eyes for a moment and pantomimed with her hands. She opened her eyes.

"Right hand," she said. "He had the gun in his right hand."

Jesse nodded.

"That would mean he's right-handed," Gloria said.

"Probably," Jesse said.

"You wouldn't carry a gun in your off hand," Gloria said.

"Probably not," Jesse said. "If he was anybody you knew, would you have been able to tell?"

"I don't think so," Gloria said. "His voice didn't sound familiar."

"Did he do anything to disguise his voice?" Jesse said.

"Like whisper or something?"

"Uh-huh."

"No," Gloria said. "That would mean he wasn't someone I might know."

Jesse grinned at her.

"Ah, come on, Mrs. Fisher," he said. "Could you let me do a little of the police work?"

"But," she said, "if we didn't know each other, he would have no reason to disguise his voice. Doesn't that make sense?"

"It does," Jesse said. "Is there anything else you can tell us?"

"Not really," she said. "He was only here, probably, a couple of minutes."

"You're a brave woman," Jesse said.

"I didn't know I was going to be," Gloria said. "But . . ."

She looked at Molly.

"You got kids?" she said.

"Yes."

"Daughter?"

"I have a daughter and three sons," Molly said.

"I just have the one daughter," Gloria said. "I kept thinking of her when I saw him. I knew who he was as soon as I saw him, you know? I'd heard about the other women. And I . . . kept thinking of my daughter . . . and I couldn't let her mother be forced to strip naked in her own living room in front of some stranger . . . I couldn't. I would not."

She looked at Molly again.

"Could you?" she said.

"I won't know unless it happens," Molly said.

Gloria nodded.

"We'll leave Officer Friedman here," Jesse said. "Until your husband gets home."

"Thank you," she said.

Driving back to the station, Jesse said, "Tough woman."

"Yes," Molly said. "I wonder if I'd have done what she did?"

"You were right when she asked you," Jesse said. "No way to know until you're in the situation."

"I hope I'd be like her," Molly said.

"Be a good woman, and a good cop, Moll," Jesse said. "Whether you did or not."

"Thank you," Molly said.

"That's what you are," Jesse said. "And whatever you do in one specific situation doesn't change what you are."

"Even what I did with a certain Native American person?"

"Even that," Jesse said.

# 36

The weather was pleasant, so Jesse took his first drink of the night out onto his balcony and sat and reread his new letter from the Night Hawk.

**Dear Chief Stone,**

**By now you must know of my recent humiliation. The woman defied me. And I had to run. Run away! I don't know why I didn't force her to do what I said. I wanted to, God knows. But somehow I seemed frozen by her. I couldn't approach her. I wanted in the worst way to take her and strip her clothes off. But**

I didn't. For reasons I don't understand I fled, and am now in my home, frightened and enraged. What I wanted to do frightens me. That I couldn't do it enrages me. And it is the rage that I really fear. I have never felt such rage. To be denied like this and humiliated in the process. It will drive me. I can feel it driving me, and if you do not stop me, I don't know what it will drive me to. I am becoming ever more dangerous. What started out as a basically harmless adventure is turning into something monomaniacal. Something—shall I say it? Yes!—something evil. So be warned, and be alert!!!

**The Night Hawk**

Jesse read it twice more. It seemed to him more a display of bravado than a call for help. *To be denied what?* Jesse thought. *A photo op? He's embarrassed because the woman faced him down and he ran. He's explaining to me and himself that he's really a dangerous bastard and needs to be stopped.* Jesse's glass was empty. He stood and went back into his living room and made himself another one. He took it back out on the balcony and sat with his feet up on the rail and looked out over the dark harbor. Jesse felt some comfort in the fact that the Night Hawk had run. Maybe he wasn't so dangerous. Maybe he protested that he was because he really knew he wasn't. *But why to me? He doesn't need my approval. He needs the approval of the town.* Jesse sipped quietly at his drink. *And the chief is, for him, the face of the town.* It was a clear night, but the moon was a slender crescent, and it shed very little light. Jesse took another sip of his drink. *Approval isn't quite it,* Jesse thought. *Fear? Respect? Fearful respect?* Jesse drank again. Then he nodded to himself. *He needs us to think he's not a pathetic creep. He wants us to think he's THE NIGHT HAWK! instead of the nasty little voyeur that he knows he is.* Jesse finished his second drink and went back to the bar. As he mixed the third, he looked at his poster of Ozzie.

"Used to be simpler, Oz. Used to be whether you could go to your right and make the long throw. Used to be about could you sit on the fastball and adjust for the curve."

Everything rode on questions like that, but not life or death. Baseball was the most important thing that didn't matter that he'd ever known. Win or lose, you played again the next day, or the next year, as far ahead as you could see when you were nineteen and had an absolute cannon of an arm.

"Had a big arm, Oz," Jesse said. "Bigger than yours, to tell you the truth. Didn't have your hands. Didn't probably have your bat. Couldn't do a backflip. But I had a gun."

He took his drink back to the balcony. Sixteen-ounce glass, lot of ice, lot of soda. The warm evening made the condensation bead up on the glass and run in tiny rivulets down the side.

*Now I gotta worry about whether this guy needs respect enough to hurt one of these women.* He drank.

"I guess we have to assume he might," he said aloud in the empty stillness. "We got to assume he might."

He drank some more.

# 37

Suitcase Simpson came into Jesse's office carrying a large paper bag.

"Seth Ralston," Suit said.

He took a large Italian sandwich out of the bag and unwrapped it on Jesse's desk.

"Is that a sub I see before me?" Jesse said.

"From AJ's sub shop," Suit said. "The best."

"You have Daisy Dyke right up the street, who makes her own bread, and you're buying mass-produced submarine sandwiches at AJ's?"

"Yeah. I got one for you, if you want it."

"You bet I do," Jesse said.

Suit handed him a second sandwich, and Jesse unwrapped it on his desk.

"Seth Ralston?" Jesse said.

"And Hannah Wechsler," Suit said. "Got 'em both for you."

"And still managed to pick up some subs," Jesse said. "What have you got."

"I gotta get a Coke first," Suit said. "You want one?"

"Just some water," Jesse said.

Suit went out and returned in a minute with a Coke and a water from the refrigerator in the squad room.

"Seth Ralston lives in one of those new condos on Beach Plum Ave., near the beach."

"I know the place," Jesse said.

They both paused to eat a bite of sandwich.

"Lives there with his wife, Hannah Wechsler. She kept her maiden name."

"Kind of figured that," Jesse said.

"Been there five years. Married for seven. No kids. He's a college professor. Taft University in Walford. She used to be his graduate student. She's still in grad school, and she also teaches some night classes at Taft."

"After seven years?"

"She's been in grad school for ten," Suit said.

"Slow learner," Jesse said. "What's he a professor of?"

Suit glanced down at his small notebook.

"English and American literature," Suit said.

"And that's what she's doing her graduate work in?"

"Uh-huh. She got a master's. Now she's working on a Ph.D."

"An English professor is just the kind of guy who would use a phrase like 'cri de coeur,'" Jesse said.

"What?"

"He used it in one of his letters to me," Jesse said.

"What's it mean?" Suit said.

"Something like a cry from the heart," Jesse said.

"Latin?"

"French," Jesse said.

"Wow, no wonder you made chief."

"I looked it up," Jesse said.

"What's the missus teach?"

"Freshman English," Suit said. "On Wednesday nights."

"How 'bout him?" Jesse said.

"He don't teach any nights," Suit said. "Matter of fact, he don't seem to teach much at all."

"What's his rank?" Jesse said.

"Rank?"

"You know, academic rank," Jesse said. "Is he a professor?"

"Yeah."

"What kind?" Jesse said.

"Kind?"

"He a full professor?" Jesse said.

"I guess so," Suit said.

"That's why he doesn't teach much," Jesse said.

Suit finished his sandwich and wiped his mouth and hands on one of the napkins.

"So I'm thinking," he said, "here's a guy likes to watch. And his wife's out every Wednesday night, so I go back over all the Peeping Tom reports . . . and they all took place on a Wednesday night."

"Before he started working days," Jesse said.

"I wonder what she does days," Suit said.

"Maybe you should find out," Jesse said. "Especially the days of the photo shoots."

"Great idea," Suit said. "Another reason you're the chief."

"I'm chief," Jesse said, "because some years back Hasty Hathaway assumed if he hired me I'd be a useless drunk and he could run the town as he wished."

"And where's Hasty now?" Suit said.

Jesse smiled.

"Excellent point," he said.

# 38

They sat in the squad room, just the three of them, with the door closed.

"I've asked Steve to come in and run the desk," Jesse said. "Me and the rest of the guys will run the department, and you will be the Night Hawk task force."

"Me and Molly?" Suit said. "Ain't a hell of a big task force."

"I'll be involved," Jesse said. "But with a twelve-man department, how big a task force do you think we can put together."

"Besides," Molly said, "we're worth several ordinary task forces."

"There's that," Suit said.

"What did you find out about Hannah Wechsler's daytime activity?" Jesse said.

"No pattern," Suit said. "No pattern to the photo sessions, except they were all on weekdays."

"As they'd need to be anyway," Molly said. "Have to have the husband and kids out of the house."

"And no daytime obligations for Hannah," Suit said. "That I can find out about."

"I wonder if he's still peeping at night?" Jesse said.

"We've been assuming he's moved on to home invasion," Suit said.

"But it isn't necessarily either or," Molly said. "He could do both."

"Any reports of peeping?"

"No, but people don't always notice," Molly said.

"And even if they do," Suit said, "they don't always report it."

"They would now," Jesse said. "With the home invasions being talked about."

"Still," Molly said. "They might not always know. I mean, that's one of the points about peeping, isn't it? That the person being peeped doesn't know it?"

Jesse nodded.

"You have the file," Jesse said to Molly.

She patted the big brown envelope on the desk in front of her.

"Good, you keep it. Share it fully with Suit as needed, and no one else."

"You worried about the pictures?" Suit said.

"I am," Jesse said. "I don't want them circulating. These women have been through enough without having a bunch of people looking at them naked."

Suit nodded.

"You think I'd circulate them?"

"No," Jesse said. "I think you might examine them closely, as I did, but you're a good cop and a good guy. You'll be fine."

"And Molly got no interest in them, being a straight woman," Suit said.

Jesse nodded.

"Okay," Suit said. "I see that."

Jesse smiled.

"Thank you," he said. "We got no real evidence that this guy is our man."

"But you think he is," Molly said.

"Yes," Jesse said.

"The Wednesday-night thing could be a coincidence," Molly said.

"Could be," Jesse said. "But if I decide it is, where does that get me?"

Molly and Suit both nodded.

"What do we do?" Suit said.

Jesse inhaled audibly. Then he was quiet for a bit.

Finally, he said, "I think he's feeling some pressure. His last letter, after Gloria Fisher chased him away, sounded a little hysterical."

"What's he feeling pressure about?" Molly said. "He has no reason to think we're getting close to him."

"I think it's the pressure of his craziness," Jesse said. "I think he knows his behavior is obsessive, and he's afraid of where it will take him."

"And he won't be able to stop himself," Molly said.

"I think that's his fear."

"So this thing he does, because he needs to do it, because he seems to get pleasure from it, is also a torment and could lead him to disaster," Molly said.

"You've read the letters," Jesse said. "That's my sense."

"Christ," Suit said. "He's like a victim, too."

"Of himself," Molly said.

"This may be getting too deep for me," Suit said.

Molly grinned at him.

"You should be used to that," she said.

Suit grinned.

"Can I be on another task force?" he said.

"Nope," Jesse said. "You're stuck with her."

Suit nodded.

"So what's the plan?" he said.

"You guys are assigned to this full-time. I know you got lives to live as well," Jesse said, "especially you, Moll. But I'd like as much surveillance on Seth as you can do. And if he spots you, no harm to it. Just cranks the pressure a little."

They both nodded.

"And," Jesse said, "I'll start asking about him. Interview the wife, their swinger friends, academic colleagues . . . him."

"That ought to squeeze his 'nads a little," Suit said.

"Isn't that sweet," Molly said. "My task force partner. 'Squeeze his 'nads a little.'"

"Short for gonads," Suit said.
"I know what it's short for," Molly said.
"So?" Suit said. "Your point?"
"Oh, God," Molly said.

# 39

"I think I have a lead on the home invader," Jesse said when he sat down in Dix's office.

"That's what you're supposed to do," Dix said.

"Get a lead on the home invader?"

"Yeah," Dix said. "You're a cop. It's your job."

"So?"

"So it's not my job," Dix said.

"Which means what?"

"Which means for the last several weeks you've been busy telling me about the cases you're working on."

"You've been helpful," Jesse said.

"And nothing about the case I'm work-ing on," Dix said.

"Which is me," Jesse said.

"Yes."

"Being a skilled investigator," Jesse said, "I conclude that you want to talk about me."

"That's another thing you've been do-ing," Dix said. "You kid about it."

"About what?"

"About whatever it is," Dix said, "that you don't want to talk to me about."

"And kidding is a clue to that?"

"It is," Dix said. "It's a distancing tech-nique."

Jesse was quiet. He looked around the office.

"Jenn went to New York," Jesse said.

Dix sat back in his chair, clasped his hands in front of his mouth and waited, looking directly at Jesse.

"She got a job on a syndicated morning show, and she's bunking with the producer till she finds her own place," Jesse said.

"The producer is male?" Dix said.

"Yep," Jesse said. "I suppose it would be cynical to suggest that she might have been bunking with him before she got the job."

"Or it may be simply learning from experience," Dix said.

"It's her M.O.," Jesse said.

Dix nodded. Jesse shook his head.

"I don't know," Jesse said.

Dix waited.

"I love her," Jesse said.

Dix nodded.

"And," Jesse said, "she loves me . . . or at least she hangs on to me."

Dix nodded again. He had an attitudinal mode sometimes that encouraged you to follow a subject in the direction you had taken. He had another one that let you know he thought you were going the wrong way. This time Jesse knew he should pursue this topic.

"Could she hang on to me for a reason other than love?" Jesse said.

Dix raised his eyebrows slightly.

"Why would she?" Jesse said.

They were both silent. Then Jesse could see Dix decide to prime the pump.

"Think about her life," Dix said. "She has some talent, but as you said, her M.O. is to sleep with men who can advance her career."

Jesse nodded.

"So that her life may seem to her to be in the control of others," Dix said.

Jesse nodded.

"In an out-of-control life," Dix said, "what stability is there? What can she count on?"

Jesse was silent for a moment.

Then he said, "Me."

Dix nodded firmly.

"She could have that. Hell, when we were married she did have that," Jesse said.

Dix nodded.

"Hell, she could have that now if she'd stay with me," Jesse said.

"But she chooses not to," Dix said.

"Or can't choose otherwise," Jesse said.

Dix nodded.

"I'm not enough," Jesse said.

"Apparently not," Dix said.

"So we're saying that because I love her and she can count on me, she's free to fuck her way to success," Jesse said.

Dix smiled faintly and nodded again.

"How's that working out for both of you?" Dix said.

Jesse leaned back in his chair and stretched his legs out in front of him.

"The Night Hawk," Jesse said, "writes

me these letters, and when you read them they sound like they're about two people. Him and his obsession. It's like the obsession needs him to do things to satisfy it, and he does them, and it doesn't satisfy the obsession . . . and it fucks up his life."

"Do I hear an analogy being drawn?" Dix said.

"Doing what the obsession wants," Jesse said, "like, makes it more obsessive."

"Sometimes," Dix said.

"So enough is never enough."

"Never," Dix said.

"Drinking water makes you thirsty."

"Yes," Dix said.

Jesse put his hands behind his head as he leaned back.

"What a great arrangement," he said.

Dix smiled.

"God is undoubtedly an ironist," he said.

"Now what the fuck do I do?" Jesse said.

"Be good to catch the Night Hawk," Dix said.

# 40

Jesse interviewed Hannah Wechsler in her office at Taft University. She shared the room with five other teaching assistants, all of whom were scruffy. Hannah was not. She was dressed appropriately enough in an ankle-length dress and sandals, but it had the look of contrivance. Her hair was too well groomed. Her makeup was too good. She was manicured and pedicured, and her teeth were very white.

"Is Seth okay?" she said when Jesse introduced himself.

"He's fine," Jesse said. "It's another case

we're working on, and we hoped maybe you could help us."

There were three other teaching assistants in the office. They all looked at Jesse with automatic hostility. Philosophically, they were grimly in favor of the working man. In fact, of course, plumbers made them uncomfortable, and they viewed cops with suspicion.

"May I buy you some coffee?" Jesse said.

"Sure," Hannah said, "the café in the student union."

It was a short walk to the student union, a short wait for the coffee, and a short search to find a table for two.

"What's this case you're working on, Chief Stone," Hannah said. "Is it the creepy guy that takes pictures?"

"Call me Jesse."

"And I'm Hannah," she said. "Is it him?"

"In fact, it is," Jesse said.

"Have you seen the pictures?" she said.

"I have."

"And they're really naked?" Hannah said.

"Yes."

"Wow," she said. "I wonder what that's like."

"To be forced to pose naked?" Jesse said.

"Yeah," Hannah said. "That, and knowing that a bunch of cops and people you don't even know are looking at you naked."

"Not too many cops," Jesse said.

"You're trying to protect them," Hannah said.

"No need to humiliate them," Jesse said, "more than is required."

"You think they're humiliated?" Hannah said.

"Wouldn't you be?"

"Be humiliated?" Hannah said. "No, actually, I think I'd find it kind of exciting."

"Really," Jesse said.

"I know, I know. I'm not supposed to think things like that," Hannah said. "But I do, all right?"

"Okay with me," Jesse said.

"Lot of women like to be looked at," Hannah said. "If they'd just admit it."

"You think any of these women might?"

"If they are not ashamed of their bodies," Hannah said. "Are able to be genuinely in touch with their own sexuality."

"You bet," Jesse said.

"You don't think so?"

"I'm just listening," Jesse said.

"Open-shuttered and passive," Hannah said. "Not thinking, merely recording."

"Something like that," Jesse said.

"You know where that comes from?"

"The open-shuttered stuff?" Jesse said. "No."

"John Van Druten," Hannah said. "*I Am a Camera.*"

"Uh-huh."

"Sorry," Hannah said. "I've been a graduate student too long."

"I don't mind," Jesse said.

"So," she said, "Jesse. Tell me this. Are you in touch with your sexuality?"

"I was," Jesse said, "when I was a teenager. But I was afraid it would cause pimples."

Hannah smiled.

"That's not quite what I meant," she said.

"You're in touch with yours," Jesse said.

"Absolutely," Hannah said.

"You're a member of the Paradise Free Swingers," Jesse said.

Hannah looked at him silently for a moment.

"Well," she said. "You're a little more subtle than I might have thought."

Jesse nodded.

"You swing, I assume," he said.

"I do," she said. "My husband and I both do."

"Tell me about it?" Jesse said.

"Why?" she said. "Light your fire?"

"Curious," Jesse said.

"Professionally?" Hannah said.

"Sort of," Jesse said.

"What do you mean 'sort of'?"

"Well," Jesse said. "We've found a possible connection between the man who does the home invasions and the Free Swingers."

"So why isn't that completely professional?"

"Personal," Jesse said.

"And what is this connection?" Hannah said.

"Can't talk about it right now," Jesse said.

"And why choose to question me?" Hannah said.

"Well, in fact, we checked out everybody's background and found out you were studying for a Ph.D. We figured you'd be smart."

Hannah laughed.

"That shows how little you know of Ph.D.'s," she said. "But on that basis, why not talk to my husband as well? He already has a Ph.D."

"We will," Jesse said. "Just arbitrarily chose you first. We're a small department, you know."

"Or you thought because I was a woman, you could bully me," Hannah said.

"How hard have I tried that?" Jesse said.

"I'll bet you don't have any leads and you heard about the swingers, and decided to scapegoat us."

"So how's it work," Jesse said.

"No," Hannah said. "It's a free and loving human experience, and I'm not going to let you make it into something else because you don't know what else to do."

Jesse nodded.

"Anyone else we should talk with?" Jesse said.

"Absolutely not," Hannah said.

"Okay," he said. "Tell your husband, if

you would, that we'll be checking with him, too."

Hannah stood and looked scornfully at Jesse for a moment, then turned and walked away. Jesse sat quietly and finished his coffee, and then he left.

# 41

"You get anywhere with Hannah Wechsler," Molly said.

"I got a handle on who she is," Jesse said.

"She tell you about the Free Swingers?" Molly said.

"She told me it was a free and loving human experience," Jesse said.

"Everybody knows that," Molly said. "She tell you anything else?"

"She told me she'd find it exciting to have men looking at pictures of her naked."

"Okay," Molly said. "She's got a good body."

"I guess."

"You don't know?" Molly said. "You, an experienced investigator."

"She was wearing some kind of dress that looked like a garment bag," Jesse said.

"But her hair was good, and she wore makeup," Molly said.

"How'd you know?" Jesse said.

"I, too, am an experienced investigator," Molly said.

"And there is no woman in the Paradise Free Swingers club that doesn't think about her appearance," Jesse said.

"That too," Molly said.

They were alone in the squad room. The conference table had several cardboard coffee cups lying on it, the wrappers from some fast-food cheeseburgers, and a couple of french fries that had escaped by nestling under the wrappers. As they talked Jesse cleaned up the table and put everything in the corner trash can. When he finished, Molly got a wet paper towel from the washroom and wiped down the table. Then they each got a fresh cup of coffee and sat down again.

"I hate a mess," Jesse said.

Molly nodded.

"You find out anything that will help with the Night Hawk?" she said.

"No, but I didn't expect to," Jesse said. "She'll tell her husband that I talked to her. If he's our guy, it may pressure him a bit."

Molly grinned.

"Squeeze his 'nads, so to speak," she said.

"Wow," Jesse said. "Moll, you're really getting the lingo."

"Makes me proud," she said.

"You keep being a cop, you may turn into a guy," Jesse said.

Molly had very big, dark eyes. She looked right at Jesse and batted her eyelashes.

"You think so?" Molly said.

Jesse smiled.

"No, Molly," he said. "I don't think so."

"Me either," she said.

"But if you're ever looking for a free and loving human experience . . ." Jesse said.

"I'll call you first," Molly said. "What are you going to do about Seth Ralston?"

"I'm going to talk all around him. I'm going to interview everybody in the swingers club. I'm going to interview his colleagues. I'm going to study his academic record.

I'm going to read his doctoral dissertation. I'm going to check his driving record."

"But you're not going to speak to him," Molly said.

"Nope."

"And you're not going to accuse him of anything," Molly said.

"Nope."

"And you'll be very careful not to say anything to indicate that he's suspected of anything," Molly said.

"Careful," Jesse said.

"But you'll buzz around his life like a big green fly," Molly said. "And drive him crazy."

"That's my plan," Jesse said.

"And the Paradise Free Swingers?"

"Maybe I can find a way to make things work better for the Clark kids."

She held her coffee cup in both hands in front of her mouth, watching the faint wisp of stream rise from it. Then she sipped some, and put the cup back down on the tabletop.

"That's diabolical," Molly said.

Jesse grinned at her.

"There's more than one way," he said, "to squeeze a 'nad."

# 42

It was Wednesday night. Jesse sat with Suit in Suit's truck, outside Seth Ralston's condo.

"So if you want him to know we're watching him," Suit said, "how come we don't use a cruiser?"

"I figure this way," Jesse said, "we have two chances. He spots you and it inhibits him, and squeezes him a little more. He doesn't spot you and you may be able to catch him in the act."

"Of what?" Suit said. "Peeping? I thought he'd moved on to his day job."

"We don't know that he's not night and day," Jesse said.

"Hell," Suit said. "We don't even know it's him. All we got is that his wife works Wednesday nights."

"And he's in a swingers group," Jesse said. "And he likes to watch."

"Hell," Suit said. "Just for the sake of discussion. Wouldn't that be true of any member of a swingers group?"

"That they like to watch?" Jesse said. "I don't know."

"Well," Suit said, "it sure don't mean that you like to keep things private."

"True," Jesse said. "It doesn't have to be Seth."

"On the other hand," Suit said, "who else we got?"

Jesse smiled and nodded slowly.

"There you have the essence of police work," he said.

"And there he is," Suit said.

Seth Ralston came out of the front door of his condo unit. He was wearing black pants and a white T-shirt. He had a Yankees cap on his head, and a dark windbreaker tied around his waist.

"Making a foray?" Suit said.

"Dressed for it," Jesse said. "Put on the jacket, zip it up, and you're all in black."

Ralston walked to the sidewalk and looked back at the truck. He paused. Then he turned and walked toward downtown.

"Drive or walk," Suit said.

"One of each," Jesse said.

Jesse got out of the car and walked in the same direction as Ralston, on the other side of the street. Suit put the truck in gear and drove past Ralston. Ralston would probably make them, Jesse knew, if he hadn't already. It was nearly impossible to tail somebody in a town the size of Paradise, with so little foot traffic. Still, it would crank up the pressure, maybe. And it was something to do.

Ralston walked slowly along Front Street with the harbor on his right. He passed Suit's truck, parked at a hydrant. He glanced at it but kept going. Jesse drifted along behind him. At the town wharf, Ralston turned and went into the Gray Gull. Suit pulled into the parking lot on the wharf and sat in his truck. Jesse went on into the Gray Gull and spotted Ralston at the bar. Jesse went to the other end of the bar and ordered a beer. He drank it slowly, while Ralston had a martini, paid, stood, and went out. Jesse left a bill on the bar and went out after him.

With Jesse watching him and Suit circling slowly in the truck, Ralston walked back to his condo and went inside. Suit parked across the street. Jesse went over and got in the truck.

"Is police work exciting," Suit said, "or what?"

"I think he was going out to peep," Jesse said, "and spotted us and changed his plan."

"Or maybe he just wanted a drink," Suit said.

"Who do you know goes out at nine o'clock at night, walks to a bar, has one martini, and walks home."

"Most people I know drink beer," Suit said. "But you got a point. It is like he was going out for another reason and changed his mind when he saw us."

"That's my theory," Jesse said.

"Kinda thin," Suit said.

"Kinda?" Jesse said.

# 43

Jesse made himself a drink and sat at the bar in his living room to read the Night Hawk's letter.

**Dear Jesse,**
   **I'm feeling trapped and desperate. No, not because of anything you're doing (God! Small-town cops). . . . No, I feel trapped by my obsession. The struggle between my obsession and my self is the real struggle, not the pathetically unequal conflict between you and me. It's not what you do or who you talk to. . . . It's whether my obses-**

sion drives me to do things that I don't want to do. It's whether finally, to save me from my obsession, I allow you to catch me and put a stop to it. . . . But I worry that if that time comes, you and the other Keystone Kops won't have the wherewithal to do it. One thing is certain: I will strike again, and you can't stop me, and can never stop me . . . unless I arrange for you to stop me in order to stop my obsession . . . It should be interesting.

**The Night Hawk**

Jesse put the letter on the bar. He stood and carried his drink to the French doors and looked out at the harbor. He drank some scotch.

*It's him,* Jesse thought. *He's letting me know that it's him. He knows I've talked to his wife. He knows we've had him under surveillance.* "It's not what you do or who you talk to." *He's letting me know. I wonder if it's conscious?*

Jesse had some more scotch.

**I wonder what it means that he called me Jesse? He's getting more ragged, I can hear it in the voice in the letter. I**

**wonder if he started out to go peeping, a deescalating step, so to speak. Maybe he'd been frightened by Gloria Fisher. Maybe he's got to back up and start over and work himself up to it again.**

Jesse walked back to the bar and made another drink.

*The trick will be,* Jesse thought, *to put enough pressure on him to make him give himself away but not enough pressure to make him hurt somebody.*

He wondered if Dix could help. He knew one thing. Dix would draw the analogy. The Night Hawk was clinging to an obsession that he felt he couldn't live without, and it was destroying him. Dix would direct Jesse's attention to his own situation with Jenn.

"It's not exactly the same," Jesse said as he walked back across his living room to look out at the harbor again. "But you don't have to bend it too much to make it fit."

Everyone wanted him to give up on Jenn. As far as that argument went, everyone was probably right. He'd be better off without her. He was pretty sure that the Night Hawk wanted to stop being the Night

Hawk. Except that he also didn't want to give up being the Night Hawk.

Jesse looked out at the harbor, except that he didn't see it. What he saw was himself in the darkened glass. Not old yet, still in shape. The booze didn't show yet.

He'd had a lot of women. They had been, by and large, good women. Sometimes amazingly good, like Sunny Randall. And he'd liked them all, especially Sunny Randall. But they weren't like Jenn.

Jenn wasn't good. Maybe that was her charm. Maybe what made their relationship so intense was the anger. Maybe when they did make love it was seasoned with rage, and the rage made it special.

Maybe he was drunk.

He walked back to get some more scotch. At the bar he made a new drink, and turned and looked back at the window where he'd been reflected and raised his glass.

"Sooner or later," he said aloud, "I'll bust you."

He drank. And looked at the black window. Was he talking to the Night Hawk, or was he talking to himself? He felt sad for the Night Hawk. Sad for himself.

"So what am I," Jesse said, "a Day Hawk? How about a Night Eagle?"

He laughed. It was a derisive sound in the empty room.

"Night and day," he sang, "I am the one."

He raised his glass toward the dark glass in the French doors that opened onto his deck.

"Only me beneath the moon and under the sun."

He drank again.

*God,* he thought, *I'm drunk.*

He walked into the bedroom, where Jenn's picture still stood on the night table by the bed. He looked at it for a moment and shook his head. Then he turned it face-down on top of the nightstand and drank some scotch.

# 44

Jesse had coffee with Sunny at the Gray Gull, which was now closed for renovation. They sat at the bar and watched Spike unload a large stainless-steel refrigerator from a truck and carry it the length of the restaurant.

"Yikes," Jesse said.

"Spike is very strong," Sunny said.

"I would have guessed that," Jesse said.

"He looks like sort of a big lovable bear, and sometimes people misjudge that," Sunny said.

"That's probably an error," Jesse said.

"Plus," Sunny said, "he does some martial-arts training."

"Like he needs to," Jesse said.

"Plus, he's really quite quick on his feet."

Jesse nodded.

"If I ever have trouble with Spike," Jesse said, "I think I'll rely on gunplay."

"Use a big caliber," Sunny said.

Jesse grinned.

"Besides," Sunny said, "you won't have trouble with Spike."

"Because I'm the chief of police?" Jesse said.

"Because you're my friend," Sunny said.

"You still painting?" Jesse said.

"Not since Rosie died," Sunny said.

"But you will," Jesse said.

"I hope so."

"Might you buy a new Rosie?" Jesse said.

"I don't know," Sunny said. "I invested so much time in her. I was married when Rosie was a puppy. . . . Now I live alone. . . . I don't know."

Jesse nodded.

"Richie's wife have the kid yet?" he said.

"Two more months," Sunny said.

"That does not bode well for your relationship," Jesse said.

"Hardly," Sunny said.

Jesse got up and went behind the bar and got the coffeepot and poured them both some more coffee.

"Maybe it's time to move on," Jesse said.

"You can say that to me?" Sunny said.

"I know."

"For crissakes," Sunny said. "You've been hanging on for years to an ex-wife who sleeps around."

"I know," Jesse said.

"And you're telling me to move on?"

"Maybe we both should," Jesse said.

Sunny leaned back on her bar stool and stared at Jesse. Then she smiled.

"We do appear to be running out of options," she said.

"You still seeing that shrink?" Jesse said.

"Dr. Silverman," Sunny said. "Yes. You?"

"I still talk to Dix," he said.

There was a half-pint carton of half-and-half on the bar. Jesse added some to his coffee and stirred in sugar. Sunny had her coffee black, with Splenda.

"You know about my Peeping Tom house invader," Jesse said.

"Calls himself the Night Hawk?"

"Yes."

"Pathetic, isn't it?" Sunny said. "The B-movie, comic-book names some of these guys come up with to make themselves seem heroic?"

Jesse nodded.

"He writes me letters," Jesse said.

"Oh," Sunny said. "One of those. I had a guy like that."

"Spare Change Killer?" Jesse said.

"You followed the case," Sunny said.

"As much of it as the media got right," Jesse said.

Sunny shook her head.

"Poor jerk . . . like so many of them, an obsessive loser. But he did such damage."

"They do," Jesse said. "My guy less than yours. He hasn't killed anybody. But . . ."

"He might," Sunny said. "But even if he doesn't, those women he's forced to strip will not be quite the same again."

"No," Jesse said.

"So why are we talking about this?" Sunny smiled. "You need help?"

"Probably," Jesse said. "But here's this guy doing something to make himself feel good, and it makes him feel bad. But he can't give it up."

"That's why we call it obsessive," Sunny said.

"Thank you, Doctor," Jesse said. "But what strikes me is that we're doing the same thing."

Sunny nodded slowly, thinking about it.

"Our efforts to be happy make us unhappy," she said.

"And yet we keep at it," Jesse said.

Sunny nodded some more.

Then she said, "That's why we call it obsessive."

"And maybe that's why we should stop doing it," Jesse said.

"If we can," Sunny said.

"We can," Jesse said.

"We almost made it once before," Sunny said.

"Remember the dress shop in Beverly Hills?" Jesse said.

"In the changing room?" Sunny said.

"Standing up?" Jesse said.

"I think standing up doesn't do it justice," Sunny said.

"We were amazingly agile," Jesse said.

"Maybe we can regain that agility," Sunny said.

"I hope so," Jesse said.

# 45

They were in the squad room.

"There was another Peeping Tom reported," Molly said.

"Wednesday night," Jesse said.

He looked at Suit.

"Never moved out of his house that I could see," Suit said.

Jesse looked back at Molly.

"I went down and talked with her," Molly said. "She looked out of her bedroom window, saw him standing in her backyard. Same outfit. All black, baseball cap. She yanked her shade down, yelled for her husband. Husband ran out into the back-yard, but the guy was gone."

"What does the victim look like?" Jesse said.

"Tall, blonde, maybe fifty-five, maybe more."

"Different than the people he photographed," Suit said.

"The peeping is probably pretty much a matter of opportunity," Jesse said. "The photography he plans ahead."

"Could be a copycat," Molly said.

"It's him," Jesse said.

"You know that how?" Suit said.

"It's him," Jesse said. "He's retrenching."

"Retrenching?" Molly said.

"Backing up and starting over," Jesse said. "Building his nerve back up."

"I was sitting out front of his condo when the peeping happened," Suit said. "He never came out."

"By the front," Jesse said. "He spotted us out front the other night."

"I know," Suit said. "So after Moll told me about the peeping incident, I went back there and looked around. And of course there's a back way out. From the cellar. Through the parking lot in back, some trees, and there's the railroad tracks. Run right on to Sea Cliff Station. Then Preston, and downtown. He'd be free and easy walking along there."

"Well," Jesse said, "he's back in business."

"And at a less intrusive level," Molly said.

"The level will escalate," Jesse said.

"Higher than before?" Molly said.

"Maybe," Jesse said. "Poor obsessive bastard."

"Poor bastard him?" Molly said. "How about the women?"

"Them too," Jesse said.

Molly said, "I don't know how you can . . . Oh."

"Anyway," Suit said. "Gives us a better shot at him. If he keeps doing it long enough, we'll catch him."

"He'll keep doing it," Jesse said. "He has to."

"Be good if we could catch him before it gets too escalated," Molly said.

"The amount of escalation will depend on the amount of resistance he encounters," Jesse said.

"You mean if a woman puts up a struggle?" Molly said.

"Pressure builds," Jesse said. "And there's no release. . . ." He shrugged.

"What if we blanket him with surveillance?" Molly said.

"I don't have the people for it," Jesse said. "Front, back, on foot, twenty-four hours a day, it would take the whole department."

"I'll bet some of the guys would work overtime," Molly said.

"Our job is to police the town," Jesse said. "Which means the whole town. Not just the Night Hawk. We still have to control traffic and answer burglar alarms and nine-one-one calls."

"How about we search his place," Suit said. "We know there's physical evidence. The gun he uses on the home invasions, the digital camera. There's probably a ton of pictures on his computer."

"There's not a prayer we could get a warrant," Jesse said.

"I might slip in without one, unofficially, of course."

"Suit," Jesse said. "We already know it's him. We need to be able to prove it, and any evidence you got while B-and-E-ing his pad would be useless to us, probably forever."

"Damn," Molly said. "This guy is committing crimes regularly. We know it. We know who he is. We know he's going to keep doing it."

"And we can't do a fucking thing about it, excuse me, Moll," Suit said.

"Clean up your fucking language," Molly said.

All three of them laughed, glad to break the tension they'd been building.

"So what do we, for crissakes, do?" Suit said.

"We await developments," Jesse said.

"'Await developments,'" Molly said.

"That, too," Jesse said, "is police work."

They were quiet for a moment, sitting around the conference table.

Then Molly said, "He only peeps on Wednesday nights."

Jesse said, "Yes."

"How many people you think we'd need to pen him up one night a week," Molly said.

"Three," Jesse said. "One out front on foot, one out back on foot, one out front in a car."

"I bet we can do it with two," Molly said. "Suit's in back on foot, with his car handy.

I'm out front in a car. He moves on foot out front and I get out of the car. He moves in the car and I follow him in my car and call Suit."

"Who jumps in his car," Suit said, "and joins the tail. I like it."

Jesse nodded.

"Could work," he said, "if you're quick."

"Who's quicker than me and Moll?" Suit said.

"Could make him move to days," Jesse said. "And escalate quicker."

"You got a better idea?" Molly said.

"I don't have one as good," Jesse said.

# 46

Steve Friedman called Jesse from the front desk.

"Got a kid here wants to see you," he said.

"Kid have a name?"

"She won't tell me," Steve said.

"Bring her in."

In a moment Steve appeared in the doorway with Missy Clark.

"I'll see her alone," Jesse said.

Steve shrugged and went back to the desk. Missy came in.

"Close the door if you wish," Jesse said.

She did. Then she came and sat where

she'd sat before. Today she was wearing a short denim skirt, a cropped pink tank top, and flip-flops. Her toenails were painted black, and there was a gold ring in her navel.

"Want coffee?" Jesse said.

"Yes, please."

Jesse poured her some.

"Milk and sugar?" he said.

"Yes, please, two sugars."

He added the milk and sugar and gave her the cup. She sipped a little.

"Hot," she said.

"Often is," Jesse said.

He poured himself some and sat back down behind his desk. She looked at the picture of Jenn for a moment. Then at Jesse.

"My parents are fighting awful," she said.

Jesse nodded.

"You talked to my mom about swinging."

"I did," Jesse said.

"Did you tell her about me?"

"No."

She continued to look at him.

"That's what they're fighting about," Missy said.

Jesse waited.

"Me and Eric can hear them," Missy said. "He comes in my room sometimes. It scares him. He wets the bed sometimes."

"Are they fighting about swinging or fighting about her talking to me?" Jesse said.

"She wants to stop. She says that you know, and that scares her. She says if you know, pretty soon everybody will know. He says it's not illegal and if she'd learn to keep her stupid mouth shut, nobody would know anything. She says she doesn't like doing it anyway. And he says that if she won't do it, he'll find somebody who will."

Jesse was quiet for a moment.

Then he said, "Well, doesn't that suck."

She had on too much inexpert makeup, which looked especially garish, Jesse thought, on a thirteen-year-old kid. Her eyes filled with tears, but she didn't quite cry.

"I don't know what to do," she said.

"Can you talk to either of them?" Jesse said.

"No."

"Why not?"

"Everybody's afraid of my father," Missy said.

"Your mother, too?" Jesse said.

"Yes."

"Does he ever hit you?"

"Not very often."

"Now and then?" Jesse said.

"Yes."

"Your mother, too?"

"Yes," Missy said.

"Well, we got a problem to solve," Jesse said.

"I didn't know who else to talk to," Missy said.

"I'm the right guy," Jesse said.

"So what are we going to do?"

"First we have to face up to them," Jesse said.

"Me?"

"You," Jesse said. "And me. I'll ask them to come in and when they do, I'll have to be able to talk about you and your brother."

"They'll know I talked to you," Missy said.

"Very likely," Jesse said. "I can soften the spin, probably. But they'll know we've talked."

"No," Missy said. "You promised."

"I can't keep them from being mad," Jesse said. "But I can pretty well guarantee that no one will harm you."

"My mom wouldn't harm me," she said.

"And I can see to it that your father doesn't."

"No," Missy said. "You can't. I got no place to go."

"And how's it going where you are now?" Jesse said.

"I . . ."

"Nothing's going to change," Jesse said, "unless we make it change."

Missy began to cry. Jesse was quiet until the crying slowed.

"It's awful," he said. "I won't pretend it isn't. And I won't pretend it's easy. But it's a chance. Otherwise, it'll destroy you and your brother. You doing dope yet?"

She shook her head.

"I won't go ahead without your okay," Jesse said. "But I think we can fix it."

"You just want to talk with them?"

"Yes."

"Do I have to be here?" Missy said.

"No."

"What if I wanted?"

"Then you'd be welcome," Jesse said.

"I don't want to," Missy said.

"Okay," Jesse said.

Missy was still sniffling. Jesse handed her a paper towel. She did what she could with it, and got her breathing steadier, and took a deep breath.

"You can go ahead," she said.

"Be a little while," Jesse said. "Till I get the ducks in a row."

"Ducks?" Missy said.

"Just an expression," Jesse said. "Hang on for a couple more days."

She nodded. They were quiet. Missy seemed as if she didn't want to leave.

"I wish you were my father," she said finally.

"Yeah," Jesse said. "Kinda wish I was, too."

# 47

"He came into my house in the early evening," Betsy Ingersoll said. "I had come home from school. Jay was working late, as he often does, and the man had a gun."

She sat in front of Jesse's desk, immaculate in a mauve pantsuit. Her husband sat beside her, immaculate in a gray suit. Molly sat in a chair in the corner nearest to Jesse. Jesse waited.

"He pointed the gun at me. He had on a ski mask, and a hat pulled low, and you can imagine how terrified I was."

"I can imagine," Jesse said.

"He came right up to me and put the

gun right against my neck"—she pointed at the little hollow at the base of her throat—"right here . . . And he told me to take off my clothes. . . . I thought of Jay, and all the children at school. . . . And I said I wouldn't, and he hit me across the face with his hand, and told me that if I didn't he'd kill me."

Jesse nodded.

"So I did," Betsy Ingersoll said.

Jesse glanced at Jay Ingersoll. Ingersoll's face was tight and impassive.

"And, and . . . he touched me."

"Intimately?" Jesse said.

"Yes. He, ah, fondled me."

Jesse nodded.

"Then he stopped and backed away and took out a camera and made me stand there while he took my picture."

She put her face in her hands and her shoulders shook slightly, but she didn't actually cry. Then she raised her face.

"Then he tied me up on the couch," she said. "And he left. When he was gone I was able to wriggle myself loose and call the police."

"You got dressed first," Jesse said.

"Yes, of course."

"And Officer Maguire came," Jesse said.

"Yes."

"Could you recognize anything about this man?"

"Oh, it was the Night Hawk, all right," she said.

"But you couldn't recognize him otherwise," Jesse said.

"She already told you he was masked," Jay Ingersoll said.

"Of course," Jesse said. "Could you tell me about the gun, Mrs. Ingersoll?"

"I don't know anything about guns," she said.

"Was it sort of blue-black, or was it sort of silver?" Jesse said.

"I don't know. It happened so quickly. I was terrified. It was just a gun."

"Of course," Jesse said.

"I might remark, Stone," Jay Ingersoll said, "that if you had worked as hard on the Night Hawk business as you did on an innocent mistake my wife may have made while trying to do her job, maybe you'd have this pervert behind bars where he belongs."

Jesse shrugged.

"You never know," he said.

"I'm particularly convinced," Ingersoll said, "that you certainly would never know."

"Small-town cop, Mr. Ingersoll," Jesse said. "Small-town cop."

"That's apparent," Ingersoll said.

"You didn't see his car or anything, did you, Mrs. Ingersoll?"

"How could I see his car?" she said. "I was tied up on the couch."

Jesse nodded.

"It's just that Officer Maguire made no mention of seeing any rope or anything."

"Of course not," she said. "When I got loose, I threw it away. I'm very neat, Chief Stone. And I had no sentimental attachment to it."

Jesse nodded.

"I'm sure you didn't," he said.

"About this, ah, groping," Jesse said. "Could you talk about that a little more?"

Betsy Ingersoll looked at her husband.

"That's enough, Stone," Jay Ingersoll said. "I'm not going to let her be further traumatized while you go all over this for your salacious pleasure."

From her chair in the corner, Molly said, "Hey."

Jesse made a stop gesture at her.

"Are you speaking as her husband or her attorney," Jesse said to Ingersoll.

"Attorney," Ingersoll said.

"Okay, Counselor," Jesse said. "It's your call."

"It is," Ingersoll said. "And I can do without any kibitzing from your subordinate in the corner."

"Everyone can," Jesse said.

Ingersoll stood and took his wife's arm. She stood with him.

"Keep me informed," Ingersoll said, and they walked out.

# 48

"That sonovabitch," Molly said.

"Jay Ingersoll?"

"Asshole," Molly said.

"He does have a nice, easy way about him," Jesse said.

"I was married to him," Molly said, "I'd run off with the Night Hawk."

Jesse smiled and nodded.

"He's very important," Jesse said.

"He implied you were after sex details because they turned you on."

"I believe he did," Jesse said.

"And that you were incompetent."

Jesse nodded.

"He was, like, mad at you about this," Molly said.

"And his wife," Jesse said.

"Yeah, and me, for crissakes."

"Insufferable," Jesse said.

"Doesn't it make you mad?"

"I was thinking about other stuff," Jesse said.

"Like what?"

"What do you think of her story?"

Molly paused in mid-anger.

"Her story," she said.

"Yep."

Molly sat back a little and thought about it.

"He hit her," Molly said.

Jesse nodded.

"He fondled her," Molly said.

"Uh-huh."

"And"—Molly began to speak fast—"he tied her up."

"Uh-huh."

"If I wasn't so busy being outraged at Jay Ingersoll, I'd have noticed that right away."

"True," Jesse said.

Molly was quiet again, rolling it around in her head.

"The Night Hawk never touched them," Molly said.

"Correct," Jesse said.

"So either the Night Hawk has changed his approach, or it's a copycat. . . ." Molly said.

"Or . . ." Jesse said.

Molly frowned.

"Or?" she said.

Jesse waited.

"Or she made it up," Molly said.

Jesse nodded.

"And she didn't know the details," he said.

"Which is why we never released the details," Molly said. "So if there was a copycat or something, we'd know."

"Yep," Jesse said.

Molly grinned at him.

"We're pretty smart," she said.

"Sure," Jesse said.

"You think she made it up?"

"Maybe," Jesse said.

"Why?"

"Husband?" Jesse said.

"To get his attention?"

"Maybe," Jesse said. "Maybe the civil suit about the panty patrol."

"Sympathy?" Molly said.

"Maybe."

"Or it could be a copycat," Molly said.

"It could."

"Or the Night Hawk could have escalated," Molly said.

"I hope not."

"What about the pictures?" Molly said. "Unless it's the Night Hawk, there shouldn't be a picture sent."

"Public knowledge," Jesse said. "The women talked about it. The press picked it up. Anyone would know to send pictures."

"And the letters?"

"Less public," Jesse said.

"So you might get a picture, but unless it's the Night Hawk, you shouldn't get a letter."

Jesse nodded.

"And if she made it up, you shouldn't get either," Molly said.

"Unless she took one herself," Jesse said.

"Who would do that?" Molly said.

"Someone who had made this all up in the first place," Jesse said.

"And would send it to you?"

"This is the woman who conducted the

great thong search," Jesse said. "We don't know what's driving her."

"I don't believe it," Molly said.

"Me either," Jesse said. "It's a hypothesis, like the escalated Night Hawk or the copycat. We'll test them all."

"Wow," Molly said, "like high school physics, the scientific method."

"And Ingersoll thinks we're just small-town cops," Jesse said.

# 49

Spike reopened the Gray Gull on a Thursday night, and Sunny Randall drove up and had dinner there with Jesse. They sat at the new and larger bar, and ordered from the new and expanded bar menu.

"You're having a martini," Sunny said.

"I am."

"I don't think I've ever seen you drink anything but scotch."

"Sometimes I just don't give a damn," Jesse said.

Sunny smiled. She raised her own glass, and they touched rims.

"Change is good," she said.

They drank.

"I tell you about this kid I'm trying to help," Jesse said.

"Missy?" Sunny said. "Her parents are swingers?"

"That's the one," Jesse said. "The mother hates swinging but does it because the father insists. The father hits Missy, and also Missy's mother. The younger brother is terrified and wets the bed."

"For which the father probably smacks him, too," Sunny said.

"Probably," Jesse said.

"Time for an intervention," Sunny said.

"Yeah, I'm having them in next week."

"Kids, too?"

"No."

"Good idea," Sunny said. "They'll have less reason to pretend."

"What are you after?" Sunny said.

"At the meeting?"

"Uh-huh," Sunny said. "You think you can get the father to straighten up and fly right?"

"No," Jesse said. "But first I'll get a sense of how bad he is—all my information on him is secondhand."

Sunny nodded.

"And if he's as bad as he sounds," Jesse said, "maybe I can scare him into behaving better."

"At least you'll have firsthand experience with what he is," Sunny said. "Long as you don't expect him to turn into a better guy."

"No, but maybe I can get him to stop with the wife-swapping, and no longer hit his wife and children," Jesse said.

"That would be a start," Sunny said.

"And then maybe if he seemed less scary to her," Jesse said, "she might find her way out of the marriage."

"Clinging too long to a marriage," Sunny said, "is maybe not a good idea, huh?"

Jesse smiled at her.

"We need another cocktail," he said, and gestured to the bartender.

"Two's my limit on these," Sunny said.

"I know," Jesse said. "More than two martinis and my speech starts to slur."

"In my case I start to undress," Sunny said.

Jesse turned to the bartender.

"Make that a double for Ms. Randall," he said.

They both laughed.

"No double," Sunny said to the bartender. To Jesse she said, "It's not necessary."

"Good to know," Jesse said.

They looked at their menus for a moment, and ordered stuffed quahogs.

"I had a thought," Sunny said.

"Me too," Jesse said.

"Not that kind of thought," Sunny said.

She paused and sipped her martini.

"My sister," Sunny said, "had an affair with a terrible man, and when she wanted to break it off, he haunted her."

Jesse nodded.

"I talked to him," Sunny said. "My sister talked to him, nothing."

She ate half of one of the olives in her martini.

"He wouldn't leave her alone," Sunny said. "So finally I asked Spike to speak with him."

Jesse nodded.

"He never bothered my sister again."

Jesse glanced at Spike, who was working the room, the jovial host.

"Spike got his attention," Jesse said.

"He did."

"You think he could reason with Missy's father?"

"I know he'd be happy to try," Sunny said.

"What an interesting idea," Jesse said.

# 50

Jesse sat with Molly in the squad room. On the conference table in front of them were three photographs of naked women. Jesse took a fourth out of an envelope and laid it down beside the other three.

"Came this morning," Jesse said. "Mailed in town. No return address."

"Betsy Ingersoll," Molly said.

"In the flesh," Jesse said. "So to speak."

Molly stood and bent over the picture, studying it.

"She looks better than I would have expected," Molly said. "No cellulite, everything firm. I'm surprised."

"I'm sure she'll be pleased," Jesse said.

"Course, she's had no kids," Molly said. "That helps."

Jesse nodded.

"There a letter?" Molly said.

Holding it carefully by the edges, Jesse put a short note in front of her on the table-top. The note read:

**FYI,**
**The Night Hawk**

"That's it?" Molly said.

"Yes," Jesse said.

Molly looked at the note again.

"Ordinary paper," Molly said. "Typeface. Nothing that will tell us anything. Finger-prints?"

"I'll have Peter go over it, but it seems unlikely."

"What about all that save-me-from-myself gush," she said, "that he usually writes."

"Good question," Jesse said. "Now, don't look at the pictures again for a minute."

Molly looked out the window.

"If you were going to pose for a nude picture of yourself, what would you do?" Jesse said.

"You mean that I took myself?"

"Yes."

"Wow, you are a suspicious bastard," Molly said.

"Just testing the hypothesis," Jesse said. "What would you do?"

"Well, I wouldn't send it to you," Molly said.

"Disappointing," Jesse said. "But think about it as if you were she. Imagine you have faked this attack and are now backing it up by taking a nude picture of yourself that you'll send to the cops."

Molly stood and walked to the window and looked out at the municipal parking lot where the trucks parked, and the plow blades waited for winter.

"Well," Molly said, without turning from the window, "first I'd try out my poses in a full-length mirror."

"See how you looked best?"

"Of course," Molly said.

"Even though you're naked."

"Especially 'cause I'm naked," Molly said. "I'd know it had to be frontal nudity, or no one would believe it. But within that, there's ways to stand, and where the light falls, and do you want to emphasize your boobs, or your hips, or whatever. Any woman knows what her best assets are. Any woman knows where full-face or profile or something in between is her best look."

"Makeup?" Jesse said.

"Absolutely," Molly said. "It's credible, and I'll look a lot better."

"Hair?"

"Ah," Molly said.

She had turned from the window. She was engaged in the subject now. Her imagination was entirely invested in how to look best while naked. Jesse smiled slightly, but Molly wasn't looking at him and she didn't notice.

"Hair is a problem," she said. "It has to look a bit tousled, as if maybe you've been roughed up, or your clothes have been forcibly removed. It can't be not-a-hair-out-of-place."

"Uh-huh?"

"But," Molly said, "I would know how to tousle it so that I'd look as good as I could."

"How would you wear it?"

"If it were me, I'd have a few thick strands loose on my forehead, and the rest sort of down and fluffed around my face."

"You never wear it like that," Jesse said.

"Jesse, for crissakes, I'm a cop. If I ever wear it like that I'm off-duty."

Jesse grinned.

"I'll check with Crow," he said.

"Oh, shut up," Molly said.

"How about if you were forced to dis-robe at gunpoint?" Jesse said.

"I'd probably be too scared to think about it much. I'd just stand there and hope it was over soon, and that he wouldn't hurt me."

"No posing," Jesse said.

"Well," Molly said. "I might suck in my stomach a little."

"Okay," Jesse said. "Look at the pic-tures."

Molly walked to the table and looked down.

"She's posing," Molly said.

"Betsy Ingersoll," Jesse said.

"Absolutely," Molly said.

"That's what I think," Jesse said.

# 51

"Do you have an opinion on the, ah, swinging lifestyle?" Jesse said.

Dix smiled and leaned back in his chair, the way he did when he was considering something.

"I do," he said.

"Care to share it?" Jesse said.

"I will," Dix said, "on the condition that you then share with me some thoughts on Jenn."

"Okay," Jesse said.

"First, like so much in my work, and yours, it depends to considerable extent on who the people are."

Jesse nodded.

"In my experience most people who swing are not in a healthy love relationship," Dix said. "On the other hand, most of the people with whom I have experience are not in a healthy love relationship, or I wouldn't be dealing with them."

"So there's some self-selection going on," Jesse said.

"As in your work," Dix said.

"I'm not going to hold you to this," Jesse said. "I'm just looking to understand it."

"If I may generalize," Dix said, "swinging tends to distort sex in marriage. On the one hand, sex is a crucial part of the relationship, indeed, in many cases, the social life. On the other hand, since both spouses presumably have sex with a wide assortment of partners, and quite publicly, it trivializes sex. Sex becomes something akin to a party game."

"I see that," Jesse said.

"Sex is intricately connected with emotion," Dix said. "Which is why, say, pornography is ultimately so disappointing."

"Swingers claim that it enhances their marriage," Jesse said. "You buy that?"

"No," Dix said. "It is inconsistent with

human emotional life, as I understand it. On the other hand"—he smiled—"despite my best efforts, my understanding of human emotional life remains incomplete."

"Any thought as to why people do it?"

"Some thoughts, but the reasons are probably too various. One common reason seems to me that it allows them to be adulterous without guilt."

"Because the other spouse is doing it, too," Jesse said.

"Yes."

"And because it can be dressed up with philosophical crap, so it's not wife-swapping, it's an approach to life, among like-minded free people."

"Yes," Dix said.

"At worst, a victimless crime," Jesse said.

"Those are rare," Dix said.

"Especially if there are children."

"About that I am clear, swinging is not good for the children of swingers," Dix said.

"In any special way?" Jesse said.

"In all ways," Dix said. "It confuses the hell out of them. They're confused about boundaries and what a family is and what love means and about sex and sexuality and about where they stand in the swingers' universe."

"So I guess you disapprove," Jesse said.

"You bet your ass I disapprove," Dix said. "Tell me about Jenn."

# 52

Chase Clark was tanned, and in health-club, StairMaster shape. His blond hair was slicked straight back. He had a prominent nose, and the skin on his face was taut and smooth. He wore tinted aviator glasses, a pink polo shirt, and a bright green sweater over his shoulders, the sleeves tied loosely around his neck. The rest of him was olive Dockers and tan boat shoes. Kim Clark had on a white dress with a black pattern, a white belt, and white heels of modest height. Jesse stood when Molly brought them into the squad room and closed the door.

"Mr. Clark," Jesse said. "Jesse Stone. I assume you've met Officer Crane."

"I have," Chase said, and smiled a big, bright white smile that spoke of careful dentistry. "Hope we aren't in any trouble."

"Not that I know of," Jesse said. "How are you, Mrs. Clark?"

"Fine."

*She looks like June Cleaver,* Jesse thought. Everyone sat.

"First, let me be clear," Jesse said. "Your membership in the Paradise Free Swingers violates no law."

Chase looked at his wife as if he was startled, but he didn't say anything to her. Instead, he spoke to Jesse.

"What makes you think we belong to anything?" he said.

"Police work is boring to describe," Jesse said. "Let me simply insist that you do, and that it'll go much quicker in here if we all agree on that."

Chase looked again at his wife.

"Did Kim tell you?" he said.

"Police work is boring to describe," Jesse said.

"Well, say we do, and say you are the

standard bluenose that thinks it's horrid but wishes they could do it. So what?"

"As I said, it's in violation of no statute that I know of," Jesse said.

"So what are we doing here?"

"I wish to talk about your daughter and your son," Jesse said.

"What have they done?"

"Nothing yet," Jesse said.

"What the hell does that mean?" Chase said. "Kim, have you been blabbing to this guy?"

Kim shook her head. She seemed stiff with tension.

"If they continue to live in the home you are providing," Jesse said, "they'll do something."

"What the fuck are you talking about?"

"The swinging lifestyle, coupled with the occasional physical abuse, is ruining the lives of your children," Jesse said. "That might come under the heading of child endangerment. We might be able to find a way to take custody from you."

Chase sat back, breathing heavily.

"Who's . . . been . . . talking to you?" he said.

"Did you know your son still wets the bed?"

Chase glanced again at his wife. She had her head down, looking at the table-top.

"Wets the bed?" he said.

"Yep."

"You been talking to someone? Kim tell you this crap? That's just like something she'd say."

Kim stared at the tabletop.

Jesse nodded faintly, and took in a long breath of air.

"Your daughter came in and asked me for help," Jesse said.

Kim looked up at Jesse.

"Missy?"

"Missy," Jesse said.

"She's spoiled," Chase said. "Kim spoils her rotten, the little bitch has no idea how soft she has it."

"Are you saying that none of this is true?" Jesse said. "Or are you saying that it is true but no one should have told me?"

"I'm saying it's not your business," Chase said. "It's family business."

"And I'm saying if it fails to provide a proper environment for the children, it becomes my business."

"What are you, Mr. Fucking Guidance Counselor?"

"I am the chief of police of this town," Jesse said. "And there is only a certain amount of guff I will put up with from you."

"We're being persecuted for being sexually creative," Chase said.

"Your wife hates it," Jesse said. "She does it because she's afraid of you."

"She tell you that?" Chase said.

"Police work is boring to describe," Jesse said.

"Don't keep saying that," Chase said.

"Next time I'll have Molly say it," Jesse said.

"Her? The lady cop? What's she doing here anyway?"

"It's her case," Jesse said.

"Case? What case."

"You know what I'm doing here?" Molly said. "I'm sitting here trying not to puke listening to you."

"She can't talk to me that way."

"Can, did, probably will again," Jesse

said. "Here's the deal. I don't care about your sex life. You can have carnal knowledge of a scallop trawler for all I care, or several at a time. But if you do not provide a stable and supportive environment for your children, then I will find a way to make you."

"That's a threat," Chase said. "You goddamned threatened me. I'm gonna get a lawyer. You're persecuting us for being sexually open."

"And," Jesse said, "if you lay a hand on any member of your family, I will have you down here in a cell faster than you can say 'wife-swap.'"

"You can't do that," Chase said.

Jesse stood and put his hands on the tabletop and leaned in over Chase.

"I'm the fucking chief of police here," Jesse said. "I can do whatever I fucking want to, and I fucking will."

Chase opened his mouth and closed it. He wanted to lean back from Jesse, but he didn't want to look scared. He sat stiffly.

"Get out of here," Jesse said.

"You can't send us home like this," Kim said. "He'll hurt us."

"You should think about leaving him and taking the kids," Jesse said. "If you'd like, I'll send Officer Crane and another officer with you while you do that."

"Leave?" Chase said. "And go where, bitch? And live on what?"

"You want to leave?" Jesse said.

Kim looked at her husband and then at Jesse and back at her husband. She shook her head.

"No," she said.

Jesse nodded.

"Okay," he said, and jerked his thumb at the door.

The Clarks stood and went out. Neither of them would look at Jesse.

When they were gone, Molly said, "I better take a ride up there. He'll hurt them."

"Maybe not," Jesse said. He gestured for her to come with him and they walked to his office and looked out the window at the parking area on the apron of the fire station driveway.

"The Clarks' car, the Lexus SUV?" Jesse said.

"One they came in," Molly said. "Who's that leaning on it?"

"No idea," Jesse said.

"Isn't that Sunny's friend, the big guy, Spike, that bought the Gray Gull?"

"Might be," Jesse said.

"It is," Molly said.

Jesse smiled and shrugged.

The Clarks approached the car and stopped. Chase spoke to Spike. Spike nodded. Kim stood motionless by the passenger door, her hand on the handle. Chase said something else to Spike, and Spike turned and put his face close to Chase's. Chase flinched visibly and tried to move away from Spike toward the driver's side. For a man of his dimensions, Spike moved very quickly. He took hold of Chase's shirt front suddenly and lifted him off the ground and set him on the hood of the Lexus. Chase tried to look toward the police station. With his left hand, Spike held Chase's face steady and leaned over and appeared to whisper in Chase's ear. Chase flapped his hands aimlessly, as if he were treading water. Then Spike let him go and stepped back. Chase scrambled off the hood of the car and opened his door, and got in. Spike bowed slightly and held the passenger door open for Kim. Then he closed the door and stepped back. Chase turned the car as fast as he could, and Spike pointed at him until Chase drove away.

Molly looked at Jesse.

"You rigged that," she said.

"No comment," Jesse said.

"It's illegal as hell," Molly said.

"Undoubtedly," Jesse said.

"And I'll bet that Chase won't lay a hand on his wife and kids," Molly said.

"My bet," Jesse said.

"Still, "Molly said. "You don't mind, I'll check on them."

"We all will," Jesse said.

"You think it'll work?" Molly said.

"It's a start," Jesse said. "Maybe we can nurture it."

# 53

Suit and Jesse were playing catch in the parking lot behind the station. Suit had a first baseman's mitt, and Jesse had his old Rawlings fielder's glove, with the round red R logo stitched on the base of the thumb. Jesse's throws popped when they hit Suit's glove.

"I thought you hurt your arm," Suit said.

"Did," Jesse said.

"Well, it feels like a big-league arm to me," Suit said.

"That's because you haven't played with a big-league arm."

The ball popped again in Suit's glove.

"Jesus," Suit said. "I been playing first base in the softball league every summer since I got out of high school. And nobody throws a ball like you."

"Muscle memory," Jesse said.

"You know Harley, played defensive end for BC? He's twice your size. When he played third for us one year, his throws came across the infield and hit my glove like a boulder. But yours, they like hiss, and plane, like a fucking bullet."

"If I had to play a hundred-and-sixty-two-game season my arm would fall off," Jesse said. "Softball season is, what, thirty, forty games? Even then I have to ice my shoulder every night."

"Well, all I know," Suit said, "is the goddamned thing hums coming across the diamond."

Jesse was throwing easily, and the day was warm. But he could already feel the twinges in his right shoulder. They'd be worse tonight.

"Time," Jesse said.

They sat in the shade on the running board of one of the town trucks and drank some water.

"How's Kim," Jesse said.

"Saw her today," Suit said. "Molly and I swap off, one of us stops by every day, see how she is. After asshole Chase has gone to work and the kids are in school."

"And?" Jesse said.

"She's okay. She says he hasn't laid a hand on her since you talked to him." Suit smiled. "And Spike. Kimmy says he won't even tell her what Spike said to him."

"Any swinging?" Jesse said.

"Nope, she says he comes home pretty late from work, and she knows he's been drinking. But he doesn't say anything to her or the kids."

"She mention their sex life?"

"For crissakes, Jesse," Suit said.

"She have any plan?"

"Mostly she's numb. I think her plan is to get through the day, as best she can, you know?"

"I know," Jesse said.

They threw for another ten minutes and went back into the station house.

In his office Jesse sat at his desk and put a little neat's-foot oil on his glove. Without getting up he put the glove carefully on top of a file cabinet, then picked up the phone and called Sunny Randall.

"How's your press contacts?" Jesse said.

"I have some," Sunny said.

"Do you know that Jay Ingersoll's wife was the apparent victim of a home invasion, by the Night Hawk?"

"The big-deal lawyer?" Sunny said.

"Yep."

"The one that was involved in some sort of thing with girls' underwear?" she said.

"Yep?"

"How come I haven't heard about it? Were there pictures?"

"Yep."

"What do you want from my press contacts?" she said.

"Publicity for the event," Jesse said.

"The home invasion?"

"Yep."

Sunny was silent for a time.

Then she said, "You hate publicity."

"I do," Jesse said. "But not this time."

"Should they contact you?"

"Absolutely," Jesse said. "I am eager to tell them everything."

Again, Sunny was silent for a time.

Finally she said, "You're up to something."

"I am."

"And I'm sure you'll tell me about it," Sunny said. "Sometime."

"Of course," Jesse said.

Sunny said, "I'll make some calls."

# 54

As Jesse expected, the letter from the Night Hawk came only days after the news stories about Betsy Ingersoll's ordeal.

**Dear Jesse,**
**Who is kidding whom? I did not invade that woman's home, or hit her, or make her undress, or tie her up on the couch. I have never had anything to do with her. And you know I have never touched one of my conquests. That's not what I'm about. I didn't take a picture of her. If someone sent you a picture of her, it was not I. You know I**

do not lie to you, Jesse. I have told you what I did after I did it, and I have been open and straightforward with you, even when it was embarrassing (like running away that time). So believe me when I tell you that I had nothing to do with anything that happened to Betsy Ingersoll. Somebody else did it. Somebody else took the picture. Somebody else sent it to you. I admit I'd really like to see the picture (my obsession kicks in). Seeing a school principal naked, if she's even halfway presentable, is particularly appealing. Authority exposed. But I didn't do it, and I don't like getting blamed for something I didn't do. And I resent some copycat pretending to be me. I'm sorry for you, in a way. It increases your problems, now that you have two of us to look for. On the other hand, maybe he's stupid and you'll catch him and it'll make you look good for a little while, until I make my move again. Or maybe you won't catch either of us. You don't have much of a track record.

The Original Night Hawk
(accept no substitute)

Jesse showed the letter to Molly, in his office. She read it through slowly, and read it again.

"That's interesting about 'authority exposed,'" Molly said.

"Yes."

"You knew he'd do this," Molly said.

"I was hopeful," Jesse said.

"Which is why you were so forthcoming to the press," Molly said.

"Free flow of information is vital to a thriving democracy," Jesse said.

"Which is why," Molly said, "ever since I've known you the only thing you've ever said to the press is 'No comment.'"

"But it is said in a free-flowing kind of way."

"You believe him?" Molly said.

"He has no reason to lie, and her story has a lot of soft spots in it."

"So you believe him," Molly said.

"Yes."

"I do, too," Molly said.

"Which leaves us with another question," Jesse said.

"Did somebody else do it, pretending to be the Night Hawk? Or did she do it herself?"

"Which one do you like?" Jesse said.

Molly sat quietly for longer than Jesse had thought she would.

But finally she said, "I think she did it herself."

"Me too," Jesse said.

"So that's our theory of the case," Molly said.

"It is," Jesse said.

"Her story is suspicious."

"Yes," Jesse said.

"If she was on the stand, a good lawyer would make her look bad."

"Yes," Jesse said.

"But we'll never get her on the stand," Molly said.

"Nope."

"We don't have enough for an indictment."

"Unless she fesses up," Jesse said.

"You still think she did it because of her husband?" Molly said.

"There's tension between them," Jesse said.

"Yes."

"She mentioned how he always worked late, I recall," Jesse said.

"And she implied he didn't have much

respect for her," Molly said. "Maybe she did it to get his attention."

"As Dix would say, we don't know enough about what drives either one of them," Jesse said.

"Are you suggesting he might be in on this?" Molly said.

"He might be," Jesse said. "This could be some weird sex game they are playing with each other . . . and us."

"Christ," Molly said. "I feel like I'm serving and protecting in Sodom and Gomorrah."

"It's getting a little gamy around here," Jesse said. "Maybe it's affecting us. Maybe she did it to divert attention from the panty-patrol incident."

"This seems a little extreme for that," Molly said.

"Unless there's some sort of exhibitionism that somehow ties to her suspicion of the girls."

"God, we're in way, way over our heads," Molly said. "What are you going to do?"

"I'll ask her to come in, show her the letter, see what she says."

"Her husband will come with her," Molly said.

Jesse shrugged.

"I'll show him the letter, too," Jesse said. "See what he says."

Molly nodded. She was looking at Jesse, smiling slightly, and nodding to herself. Jesse waited.

"I've gotten to know you pretty well since you got here," she said after a while.

"Know and love," Jesse said. "I am the chief of police."

"Yeah," Molly said. "And I am pretty sure I know another reason you released all this sort of embarrassing publicity of Betsy Ingersoll."

"Which is?"

"It's her punishment for embarrassing those young girls."

Jesse smiled.

"You can't arrest her or anything," Molly said. "But you sort of balanced it out this way."

"You do seem to know me," Jesse said.

"Seem?" Molly said.

"Okay, you know me," Jesse said. "Does this mean we can have an affair?"

Molly smiled at him warmly.

"No," she said.

# 55

The conference room on the thirty-fourth floor at Cone, Oakes provided a long look out over the harbor and a good way out onto the Atlantic Ocean. Across the harbor you could see Logan Airport, and looking almost straight down, the archway that led to Rowe's Wharf. Jesse turned from the view when Rita Fiore came in.

"The view is to impress clients," Rita said.

"Impresses the hell out of me," Jesse said.

"And you're not even a client."

"Friend of the firm," Jesse said.

Rita went to a sideboard and poured them each some coffee, then sat on the conference table with her legs crossed. Jesse nodded at her legs and made a thumbs-up gesture.

"*Thumbs*-up was not quite my plan," Rita said.

Jesse grinned.

"We talked about the managing partner of the firm a while ago," Jesse said. "Now I need to know more. Tell me what you didn't tell me before."

"You're exploiting our past, if fleeting, relationship?" Rita said. "To get me to gossip about my boss?"

"Yes," Jesse said.

"What about ethics?"

"You're a lawyer," Jesse said.

"Oh, right," Rita said. "I withdraw the question. What do you need to know, off the record?"

"Does he fool around?" Jesse said.

"He's a cock hound," Rita said.

"And you know this how?" Jesse said.

Rita grinned.

"Firsthand," she said. "So to speak."

"Ahh," Jesse said. "So that's how you got to be a senior partner."

"Along with brilliant trial work," Rita said.

"You are brilliant in both arenas," Jesse said.

"You should know," Rita said.

"You think Betsy is aware?"

"I have no idea," Rita said.

"Is he careful?" Jesse said.

"No," Rita said.

"Is there a particular squeeze?" Jesse said.

"He tends to graze among the new lawyers. At the moment he's got a blonde kid from Tax and Trust that's two years out of Stanford."

"Do we know how he feels about his wife?"

"He thinks she's excruciatingly conventional," Rita said.

"That doesn't sound like love to me," Jesse said.

"Nor to me," Rita said.

"Do you know why he has stayed with her?"

"She doesn't occupy much of his time," Rita said. "He is here probably twelve hours a day, and spends a lot of his evenings and weekends with the plonk du jour."

"Plonk?" Jesse said.

"You know, as in he's plonking her?"

"Plonk," Jesse said.

"So he's not home much. There are no kids. Probably finds it convenient to have somebody cleaning the house and sending his shirts to the laundry."

"Think he plonks her?" Jesse said.

"His wife?" Rita said. "I haven't thought about it. Why are you interested?"

"I think she staged the home invasion," Jesse said.

"Staged?" Rita said.

"Yes."

"And took her own picture?" Rita said.

"Yes."

"And *cherchez l'homme*?" Rita said.

"Well, it's a theory," Jesse said.

"She's trying to get his attention?" Rita said.

"Maybe."

"Or maybe he pays no sexual attention to her, poor baby," Rita said. "And she wants to show him that someone might care to see her naked."

"Even if it's a wacko?"

Rita smiled.

"There are people who think a wacko is better than no one," Rita said.

"I've heard that," Jesse said.

# 56

"Did you know that Hannah Wechsler isn't teaching any night courses this semester?" Molly said.

"I didn't," Jesse said.

"It was bothering me that we were sitting on Seth Ralston every Wednesday night and he wasn't moving."

"I figured after he spotted me and Suit on his tail last time," Jesse said, "he was laying low again."

"I called the university," Molly said. "Hannah Wechsler is not teaching a night class this semester."

"So he can't get out," Jesse said.

"At least on Wednesday nights," Molly said.

"Do you know what she's doing?" Jesse said. "Does she teach days?"

"No," Molly said. "It took me about eight thousand phone calls, but apparently she's taking a year off to write her Ph.D. dissertation."

"So he can't count on her being out of the house on a regular schedule."

"My guess," Molly said.

"And neither can we," Jesse said.

"I'll find out if she's working at home or someplace else," Molly said. "Or both."

"Even if she's working someplace else," Jesse said, "it's voluntary. She might stay home any day, or come home early any day. You can't count on it like a scheduled class."

"So he has to practice his obsession when he has the opportunity, which may not be predictable."

"We can't stay on him twenty-four-seven," Jesse said.

"We?"

"You and Suit," Jesse said. "But I've been with you in spirit."

"That's been great," Molly said. "But

you're right. There's no point to the Wednesday-night stakeouts anymore."

"Best we, or you and Suit, can do is make random checks at unexpected times," Jesse said.

"Boy, those are great odds," Molly said.

"You got a better plan," Jesse said.

"I don't have one as good," Molly said.

Jesse smiled.

"You and Suit could watch Hannah for a week or so," Jesse said. "See if there's any pattern in what she does and where she goes."

Molly nodded.

"If he's as driven as you think he is," Molly said, "this must be pressuring him something fierce."

"Yes," Jesse said.

"What do you think he'll do?" Molly said.

"What I know is, he can't do nothing. The pressure will build. He'll have to find a way."

"You sound so sure," Molly said.

"Obsession can be tough," Jesse said.

# 57

Hannah Wechsler came into Jesse's office wearing a flowered skirt and a white T-shirt. She had on big hoop earrings and some sort of low suede boot. *Her upscale intellectual uniform,* Jesse thought.

"I need to talk to you," she said.

"Okay," Jesse said.

Molly stood in the doorway. Hannah looked at her.

"I would prefer that our conversation be private," she said.

"Okay," Jesse said.

Molly went back to the desk.

"What was she going to do?" Hannah said. "Listen in?"

"We usually ask her to be present when there's a woman alone in the office with me," Jesse said.

"Oh, for God's sake," Hannah said.

"Coffee?" Jesse said.

"No."

Jesse nodded and leaned back a little in his chair. Hannah looked around the office. Jesse's gun lay holstered on top of the file cabinet.

"There it is," Hannah said, "the inevitable gun."

"Yep," Jesse said.

"I don't like the police," she said.

"I sensed that," Jesse said.

"The visible representation of a repressive state," Hannah said.

"Me?" Jesse said.

"All of you," Hannah said.

Jesse nodded.

"Well," he said, "thanks for stopping by."

She shook her head.

"No," she said. "I . . . my husband has disappeared."

"Tell me about that," Jesse said.

"Two days ago, three if you count today,"

she said. "I came home from the library. . . .
God, I don't need this in the middle of my
dissertation."

"Must be a distraction," Jesse said.

"You have no idea," she said.

"No," Jesse said.

"I came home and there was a note on
the kitchen table."

She opened her handbag and took out
a piece of white printer paper and handed
it to Jesse.

"I'm going away for a while," it said.
"Don't look for me."

Jesse put the paper on his desk. She
looked at him. He looked back.

"Well?" she said.

"I guess he's left," Jesse said.

"Of course he's left," she said. "Can you
find him?"

"Maybe," Jesse said.

"What do you mean 'maybe,'" she said.

"Police work is uncertain," Jesse said.
"You have any thoughts?"

"Like what?" she said.

"Where he might have gone?" Jesse
said. "Why he went? How long is 'a while'?"

"No."

"Have any reason to suspect foul play?"

"No," Hannah said. "But why would he leave like that?"

"Any trouble in the marriage?" Jesse said.

"No, of course not. We were very happy."

"Anything about the Free Swingers that might be helpful?"

"Oh, naturally, all you moralistic ya-hoos, you'd love to blame it on swinging, wouldn't you?"

Jesse was resting his elbows on the arms of his chair with his fingertips at chin level. He tapped the tips of his fingers together slowly.

"I don't mean to be too repressive here," he said. "But you asked me to find your husband. To do that, I need to ask questions."

She was silent for a moment.

"As a matter of fact," she said, "we stopped going to swinger parties."

"When?" Jesse said.

"It's been several weeks," she said.

"Do you know exactly?" Jesse said.

"Not now. It's on my calendar. When I get home I can call you," she said.

"Do," Jesse said. "Why did you stop going?"

"My husband said he'd lost interest, that he was bored by it all."

"And you wouldn't go without him?" Jesse said.

She looked at him the way she might have studied a caveman.

"You really don't get it, do you?" she said.

"Guess not," Jesse said.

"Going alone is not the point," she said.

Jesse nodded.

"Has he ever left before?"

"Absolutely not."

"No arguments, nothing to precipitate it?"

"None."

"Did you argue at all about giving up swinging?"

"I wouldn't call it an argument," she said.

"What would you call it?"

"I wanted to continue," she said. "He wished to stop. We disagreed."

"Angrily?"

"No, we don't have an angry relationship," she said.

Jesse nodded.

"He take anything with him?"

"His computer's gone," she said.

"He have a car?"

"Yes, a black Chrysler Crossfire," she said. "You know, with the slanty back?"

"Plate numbers?"

"I don't know," she said.

"Insurance broker would know."

"Yes," she said. "I can get it when I go home."

"Let me know that, too," Jesse said.

"Plates and the day he stopped swinging," she said.

"Yes," Jesse said. "And a list of credit cards. He have a checkbook?"

"Yes, I think he took that, too," she said. "We each have our own separate accounts."

"We'll need the name of his bank. Account numbers if you have them."

"We have such a good marriage," she said. "Sexually compatible. Both love the academic life, love literature."

Jesse nodded.

"Well," he said. "Something happened."

"Of course it did," she said. "Seth disappeared."

"In the last several weeks he has made some major changes in his life. He quit swinging. He left you. Something caused that."

"Unless something happened to him," she said.

"Unless that," Jesse said.

"What are you going to do."

"Once we get your input we'll look for his car, check his credit-card activity, see if he's cashing checks anywhere or using ATMs, the usual stuff," Jesse said. "You'll let us know if you hear from him."

"Do you think you'll find him?" she said.

"Probably," Jesse said. "Of course, if he's left voluntarily, and broken no laws, we can't force him to come back."

"I have to know what happened," she said.

"Don't blame you," Jesse said.

# 58

"He declined to go to a swinger party," Jesse said, "two days after Gloria Fisher chased him out of her house."

They were in the squad room drinking coffee.

"Must have killed him," Molly said. "The fearsome Night Hawk."

"So why wouldn't he want to do more swinging, not less?" Suit said.

He had brought a box of doughnuts and was eating one. Jesse had already had one, and Molly had broken one in half and eaten half of it. Jesse took the discarded half.

"I don't know," Jesse said. "I don't know why he does what he does."

"And then a few weeks later he disappears on his wife," Molly said.

"May be a string of coincidences," Jesse said.

"But coincidences don't do us any good," Suit said. "They don't give us anyplace to go."

"Where'd you get that idea?" Jesse said.

"You told me that twenty times," Suit said.

"Oh," Jesse said. "Yeah."

"The good news here," Molly said, "is now we have a legitimate reason to poke around in his affairs more. Access his credit-card records, see who he writes checks to, that sort of thing."

"I'd like to find a way to look at his computer," Jesse said. "We find the pictures in there, we got him."

"Too bad he took it, we'd have had a legitimate reason to look in there, trying to find him," Suit said.

"That's why he took it," Molly said.

"If we were to find it, before we found him . . ." Jesse said.

"We might get away with it," Molly said.

"We'll keep it in mind while we're looking," Jesse said.

Jesse examined the contents of the doughnut box and selected another cinnamon-sugar.

"Moll?" he said, and offered the box.

"My God," Molly said. "Keep those away from me, you animal."

Jesse shrugged and pushed the box toward Suit. Suit took out a honey-dip and bit into it.

"Moll," Jesse said. "You got the credit-card stuff, the checking accounts, the car registration."

"Yep," Molly said. "Let the phone calls begin."

"Suit, get his license picture and take it around to the local motels," Jesse said. "Check the parking lots, too, for the car."

"Molly," Suit said. "You sure you don't want another one of these doughnuts? It's cop food. You're a cop. Get a little meat on those hips?"

Molly put her fingers in her ears and squeezed her eyes shut.

"Suit," Jesse said. "You're department liaison with the Paradise Free Swingers. They got like a president or anything?"

"Head wife-swapper?" Suit said. "I don't know. I could ask Debbie."

"Do that," Jesse said.

"And if they do?"

"I'd like to gather them together and talk with them," Jesse said.

"And if they don't?" Suit said.

Jesse grinned.

"I'd like to gather them together and talk with them," Jesse said.

"Sort of limits my options," Suit said.

Jesse nodded.

"You want all of them?" Suit said.

"Just the women," Jesse said.

Suit smiled.

"Can I be there?" he said.

"Probably be Molly," Jesse said. "She makes the women less uneasy."

"Sure, go ahead," Suit said, "eat my doughnuts, but when I need a favor . . ."

Molly grinned at Suit.

"I'll tell you what they talked about," Molly said. "It will be almost the same."

"The hell it will," Suit said.

# 59

Jenn's voice on the answering machine said, "Jesse. It's me. I know you're probably still working, but I needed to talk."

Jesse drank some from his first drink of the night.

"The program is struggling. Syndication isn't going as well as we'd hoped. They're talking about restructuring, and it could mean that there'd be no job for me."

Jesse sighed aloud in the empty living room. He took another swallow of whiskey.

"I'm scared, Jesse. I don't know what to do. I need to talk to you. I . . . I guess I need you. . . . Call me."

Jesse stared into his drink. Ice always had a nice, fresh look to it. Clean-looking. He finished the glass and made another. Full glass of ice. Two inches of scotch. Fill with soda. Stir with forefinger.

"Boyfriend must have bailed on her," Jesse said aloud.

Carrying his drink, he walked into the kitchen and looked into his refrigerator. Not much. Maybe later he'd fry a couple of eggs, make a sandwich. Maybe some onions. He took his drink back to the living room and sat down.

"And I'm the safety net," he said.

He laughed without pleasure and drank some whiskey.

"Backup," he said.

He laughed again and drank again.

"A career backup," he said.

He looked at his drink.

"It's going good," he said. "I'm on the bench. It's going bad, she calls. I rescue her."

He drank.

He looked at his picture of Ozzie Smith. He looked at his gun and badge lying on the bar. He finished his drink and stood and made another one. He walked with his drink into the bedroom and looked at the picture of Jenn on his night table. He gestured at it with his glass.

"Here's looking at you, kid," he said.

He sat on the bed, looking at her.

It would be nice to have her home. It would be nice to call her and say, *Come on home, I'll look out for you.* She enriched a space when she was in it. Her laughter bubbled. Her affection seemed genuine. She was good-looking and funny and she was smart . . . he smiled . . . though not always. If she was to come and stay with him, they'd have sex. Sex with Jenn was like sex with no one else. He knew, if he looked at it for a while, that it wasn't so much what she did, it was how he felt.

His glass was empty. Drinks disappeared faster, he noticed, the more of them you drank. He stood and walked back to the living room and mixed another. He'd been doing pretty good lately. Two drinks before dinner, maybe half a glass of wine with dinner. Tonight, not so good.

He drank.

He looked at the phone.

"You keep on doing the same thing you been doing, and expect the results to be different," Jesse said aloud. "You're maybe a little crazy."

He looked at his picture of Ozzie Smith and raised his glass toward it.

"Maybe even a little obsessive, Oz. You know?"

He drank, and looked at the phone.

Couple more drinks, maybe less, and there'd be no more pleasure to it. Then it would be something else, something dull and needful.

"But not yet," he said.

And drank.

And didn't call.

# 60

"I hope you didn't mind coming into Boston," Jay Ingersoll said in a way that let Jesse know that he didn't really care whether Jesse liked it or not.

"I didn't mind," Jesse said.

He sat across from Jay Ingersoll's big desk on the top floor of Cone, Oakes. Betsy Ingersoll sat to her husband's left in a comfortable chair facing Jesse. It was a big office, but not ornate, the most prominent features being the view, which rivaled that from the client conference room three flights down, and a large leather sofa on the inside wall next to the door.

"What can we do for you?" Jay said.

"I have a letter," Jesse said, "from the Night Hawk that I thought you both should see."

Jay Ingersoll put out his hand.

Jesse took a photocopy of the original letter from his briefcase and gave it to Ingersoll. He took another copy and started to hand it to Betsy. Ingersoll put up a hand.

"I'll read it," he said.

Jesse held on to the copy and waited.

Ingersoll read the letter carefully. His face seemed to harden, but otherwise nothing changed. He looked up at Jesse when he was through reading.

"You find this credible?" he said to Jesse.

"You?" Jesse said.

"What does it say," Betsy asked.

"It's about you," Jay said.

"Then perhaps," Betsy said, "I ought to see it."

Jesse handed her a copy.

"Don't say anything," Jay said to her.

She read slowly. As she read, her face began to flush. When she finished she stared at the paper for a moment and then looked at Jesse.

"Well, of course he tells you that," Betsy

said. "He's a perverted criminal. He wouldn't admit it."

"Betsy," Ingersoll said, "don't talk."

"I mean, do you think I made it all up, for God's sake?"

"Betsy," Ingersoll said sharply.

"Actually, ma'am, I do think you made it all up," Jesse said.

"Betsy," Jay Ingersoll said. "He is saying that you filed a false police report. That's a crime. It is time to let your lawyer do the talking."

"Oh, screw you, Jay," she said. "If you expect me to sit here and be insulted, then you can just kiss my ass."

"He's not insulting you, Betsy," Ingersoll said. "He's questioning you in the presence of your lawyer."

"Well, I want another lawyer, then," she said. "I am sick to death of you."

"The Night Hawk regularly writes me letters," Jesse said. "In every one he brags about what he has done. In this letter he denies it. He has never touched a victim. According to you, he hit you and forced you down and tied you up. In this letter he denies it. He has never sent me a letter that didn't tell the truth."

"How do you even know it's him?" Betsy said.

"I know his voice by now," Jesse said. "And who else would write, and why?"

Ingersoll stood.

"I'm afraid this meeting is over, Chief Stone," he said.

"And you'd take his word over mine?" Betsy said. "A school principal?"

"Well, your record there is not unblemished," Jesse said.

"Enough," Ingersoll said. "This interview is finished."

"She has told me you're not her lawyer," Jesse said.

"Goddamn it," Ingersoll said. "I am also her husband."

"As such, you have no standing to stop the interview," Jesse said.

"What blemish," Betsy said.

"The panty-check escapade was a little odd," Jesse said.

"Betsy," Ingersoll said.

Betsy was leaning forward toward Jesse, her shoulders hunched, her hands clasped tightly.

"Odd?" she said. "Odd that a dedicated educator would care enough about her charges that she would try to prevent these girls from growing up to be sluts?"

"Betsy," Ingersoll said. "Please, please, please, please shut up. If not for yourself, then for me."

"For you?" Betsy said.

"My reputation," Ingersoll said.

"Your reputation?" Betsy said. "Your reputation. Your reputation *is* sluts. I sit here and look at that couch and wonder how many little law-school whores you've been with there."

Ingersoll stared at her for a moment.

Then he said, "Fuck this. Hang yourself." And walked out of the office.

She screamed at him as he left.

"Whoremaster!"

Jesse sat quietly.

Betsy said more quietly, "Whoremaster."

She seemed to be speaking to herself.

"He why you faked the home invasion?" Jesse said.

"He didn't even care," she said thoughtfully. "You know what he said when he learned what happened?"

"Tell me," Jesse said.

"He said, 'If those pictures get out, I'll be laughed out of court.'"

There was a dreamy quality to the way she was speaking.

"Did he know it was a fake?"

"No," she said. "He thought it was real."

"And he didn't care," Jesse said.

"No, he didn't even want to hear about it. He seemed angry that I'd called the police."

"That must have been hurtful," Jesse said.

Betsy nodded absently.

"'Hang yourself,'" she murmured.

She seemed to be talking to herself much more than to Jesse.

"Okay," Betsy said. "I'll hang us both. See how he likes that."

Jesse nodded. Betsy took a deep breath.

"He has cheated on me since I've known him," she said.

As she spoke, some tears appeared on her cheeks.

"He had a reputation when I married him," she said.

Her voice was steady and soft.

"But he was so handsome, and I was, I guess, naively flattered that a man who had been with so many women would pick me. I assumed it was love."

"That makes sense," Jesse said.

"I thought he'd change," she said.

"But he didn't," Jesse said.

"No matter what I did," she said.

The tears came harder. "No matter what I did. No matter how hard I tried. God, I was an idiot."

"Maybe not," Jesse said.

"I tried everything. I read books on sex, I bought sexy lingerie. I tried so hard."

She looked at Jesse suddenly, as if she'd come out of a trance.

"He laughed at the lingerie," she said.

"Hard," Jesse said.

"I even went to a therapist for a while, to find out what was wrong with me."

Jesse nodded.

"Your husband must have been unpleasant about the incident at school," he said.

"I did nothing wrong," she said.

"But his reputation . . ." Jesse said.

She nodded.

"He was very angry," she said.

"And with the Night Hawk being the talk of the town," Jesse said, "you thought maybe it would distract people from the school incident, and also engage you husband's sympathy."

"I was hoping he might say something like 'Thank God you weren't harmed.'"

"But he didn't."

She shook her head slowly.

"No," she said. "He didn't."

"You knew there had to be a picture," Jesse said. "Everybody knows about the pictures."

"Yes," she said. "I did it with a timer."

"Nice job," Jesse said. "But you didn't know how he operated, because we kept that to ourselves. The fact that he never touched anyone, that his letters to me were of a particular kind."

"No," Betsy said. "I just knew about the pictures."

"The good thing about this plan," Jesse said, "was if it didn't work, and you got caught, at least he'd suffer, too."

"I didn't think of that," Betsy said.

Jesse nodded.

"Can't think of everything," he said. "Do you suppose you could come in to my office tomorrow and make a statement."

"He'll have a fit," she said.

"So?"

"Of course I will," she said.

"Thank you."

"Am I in serious trouble?" she said.

"Not too," Jesse said.

"Will I have to go to jail?"

"I doubt it," Jesse said.

"Will you bring charges?"

"I don't know," Jesse said. "I'll have to think about it."

"Thank you for your kindness," Betsy said.

"You're welcome."

"May I go?" she said.

"Yes," Jesse said. "I'll walk out with you."

They stood. Jesse took her arm and they walked past the couch to the door.

"You've seen the picture of me," she said.

"Yes."

"I'm not so unattractive," she said.

"You're quite attractive."

"Did you like seeing me undressed?"

"Yes," Jesse said.

"He doesn't even bother to look," she said.

"Whatever he does, or doesn't do," Jesse said, "it's not because of you."

"What?"

"The reason he is a womanizer is not in you," Jesse said. "They're in him."

"You seem so sure," Betsy said. "How do you know that?"

Jesse smiled at her.

"I am the chief of police," he said, and opened the door.

# 61

Jesse phoned Sunny Randall in the morning.

"You're still seeing that shrink, right?" he said.

"Dr. Silverman," Sunny said. "Yes, I am."

"So you still think she's good?"

"Very."

"Okay, I might have someone I'd like to refer to her. She taking new patients?"

"I'll ask her," Sunny said.

"What's her first name?" Jesse said.

"Susan," Sunny said. "Susan Silverman."

Jesse wrote it down.

"Got a phone number and address?"

Sunny gave him both. He wrote that down.

"How soon?" Jesse said.

"Will I ask?" Sunny said. "Today. I see her at ten. I can give you an answer about eleven."

"Good," Jesse said. "Woman's name is Betsy Ingersoll."

"The panty peeker?"

"Yep," Jesse said.

"The recent Night Hawk victim?"

"Sort of," Jesse said.

"Sort of?"

"She faked it," Jesse said.

"Faked it?" Sunny said. "Why would you want to send her to a shrink?"

"Everybody's going," Jesse said.

"Speaking of that, why not send her to Dix?"

"Too close," Jesse said. "Dix wouldn't do therapy with me and take on someone I'm involved with as a cop."

"Of course not," Sunny said. "Dumb question. Why'd she fake it?"

"Maybe to get her husband's attention," Jesse said. "Maybe other reasons."

Sunny was quiet for a moment.

Then she said, "You're going to squeeze her."

"You think?" Jesse said.

"You're going to give her a choice between being arrested for filing a false police report and going to see a shrink."

"That's correct," Jesse said.

"You're a good guy," Sunny said, "but I'm not sure you're that good. She strike a nerve?"

"She did," Jesse said.

"Which you don't care to discuss with me," Sunny said.

"Not at the moment."

"But which has something to do with Jenn," Sunny said.

"Stop showing off," Jesse said.

"That's a no-brainer," Sunny said. "Everything has something to do with Jenn."

"Some things change," Jesse said.

"And some things don't," Sunny said. "I'll call you after I see Dr. Silverman."

# 62

Suit and Molly came in with Betsy Ingersoll after lunch. She had on a sober blue dress and low-heeled black shoes. She wore a pearl necklace and pearl earrings. She looked like the perfect corporate wife.

"Your husband with you?" Jesse said when she sat down.

"No," she said. "He didn't come home last night."

"Is that unusual?"

"No."

"I need to tape this," Jesse said.

"That is acceptable," Betsy Ingersoll said. "But could it be just you and me?"

"Of course," Jesse said.

Molly and Suit left and closed the door behind them. Jesse turned on the tape recorder.

"This is Chief Jesse Stone, of the Paradise police. This interview is conducted in my office at Paradise police headquarters. The interviewee is Betsy Ingersoll. You ready, Betsy?"

"I'm ready," she said.

"Do you wish an attorney?" Jesse said.

"No."

"You have the right to one," Jesse said.

"I'm very, very tired of attorneys."

"If you don't know who to call, or can't afford one," Jesse said, "we can provide you with one."

"You're reading me my rights," she said.

"For the record," Jesse said, "do you waive your right to an attorney."

"I do," Betsy said.

"Okay," Jesse said. "Tell me what you told me last night in your husband's office."

She told her story as if she was giving an oral report. As she talked she didn't look at Jesse. She seemed to have picked out a spot on the wall to Jesse's right. And she stared at it as she talked. She was well prepared. Jesse didn't have to prompt her. When she finished, she shifted her gaze from the wall to Jesse and smiled and sat quietly with her hands folded in her lap. Jesse leaned forward and shut off the recorder.

"Thank you," Jesse said.

"What will you do with me?" she said.

"Depends on you," Jesse said.

"How?"

"I have the name of a very competent, highly recommended psychotherapist whom I would like you to see," he said. "She has already agreed to see you, if you'll call and make an appointment."

"You think I'm crazy," Betsy said.

"You've done some crazy things," Jesse said.

"I'm not crazy," she said.

"Not very," Jesse said. "But I think you need help working things out with your husband."

"And if I refuse?"

"I can probably get you jail time," Jesse said.

"So those are my choices?" she said. "I see your stupid shrink or you arrest me?"

"That's pretty much it," Jesse said.

"You are being very cruel," she said.

"I didn't have to offer you the shrink," Jesse said.

She shifted her gaze back at the spot on the wall to Jesse's right and sat. Jesse sat with her.

After a time she sighed and said, "What's his name?"

"Her name is Dr. Susan Silverman," Jesse said.

"She a friend of yours?"

"I've never met her," Jesse said. "A friend of mine sees her, and my own shrink recommends her highly."

"You have a shrink?"

"I do," Jesse said.

Betsy studied the wall.

"How often do I have to go," she said.

"As often as you and she decide," Jesse said. "And you have to go for at least a year."

"A year?"

"Yes."

"She decides how often during the year?"

"You and she," Jesse said.

"So the more she tells me to come, the more money she makes," Betsy said.

"Take it or leave it," Jesse said.

"Why can't you just leave me alone?"

"You can't be left alone," Jesse said. "You need help."

She began to cry. Jesse waited. This was real crying, with a lot of heaves and gasps. Eventually she got it under control enough to speak.

"You're trying to help me," she said.

Jesse nodded.

"You may be the only one who ever has," she said.

Jesse nodded.

"I'll see her," Betsy said.

# 63

Jesse made two photocopies of the letter and put the original in his evidence file. When Molly came in he gave her one copy and kept the other for himself.

They read it together:

**Hey, Jesse,**
   **Well, you don't quit. I'll give you that. You'll enjoy the swingers. They're a fun group. You probably wonder how I know you're going to talk with the swingers. Let's just say I keep in touch. One thing for sure, if you're talking with the swingers group, you must be circling in on**

me, or think you are. Maybe you'll get me one day. But if you do it won't be you that does it. You'll just be standing around when my old friend Mr. Obsession turns me in. Some shrink would probably say that I was externalizing my pathology and objectifying it by calling it Mr. O. You know anything about psychology, Jesse? Shrinks say tons of stuff like that . . . useless shit. You got any idea what it's like to have Mr. O sitting on your chest all the time? Probably not. It's like being a prisoner. I sit here and look at my pictures on my computer, and the more I look, the more they aren't enough. Mr. O needs fresh meat. Funny, isn't it? They all look about the same. They all got the same secret. But Mr. O keeps needing to discover that secret again, and again, and again. On that basis, I keep doing it, and doing it, you'll probably catch me in time. It really sucks, you know? I hate myself for what I do, but if I don't do it . . . I have to do it. The way you have to eat, or drink. Mr. O requires it. But Mr. O won't let me touch them. Is that weird, or what? It's why my wife and I joined the swingers. We didn't have sex for three years, I think, before we joined. It was exciting to look at her, but I could never perform when it came to actual touching. I didn't actually have sex with anyone at the swinger parties, either, but Mr. O is a clever bastard, and I think they didn't know that. I don't know really why I'm writing to you like this. You're a small-town cop, probably thinks Freud is a kind of antifreeze. But we're sort of comrades-in-arms. You know? We're kind of in this together. Doing some kind of dance where I lead and you follow. Be interesting to see what happens when the music stops.

"He's telling me who he is," Jesse said.

"We know who he is," Molly said.

"But he wants us to know. He's making sure."

"Then why doesn't he just say, 'My name is Seth Ralston,'" Molly said.

Jesse shook his head.

"Then he's not the Night Hawk anymore," Jesse said. "Think of this as foreplay."

Molly nodded.

"And the meeting with the swingers?" she said.

"More foreplay," Jesse said.

Molly frowned and then smiled.

"You'll say things that you want him to hear," she said.

"Try to keep the pressure on him," Jesse said. "If he stays hunkered down some-place, I won't be able to catch him."

"You think he wants you to catch him?" Molly said.

"Does and doesn't," Jesse said. "I'm try-ing to work on 'does.'"

"How do you think he knows about the meeting?"

"Probably his wife," Jesse said.

"Which means she knows where he is?"

"Or he calls her," Jesse said.

"I feel sort of bad for him, in a strange way," Molly said.

"I know," Jesse said.

"And his wife," Molly said.

"Yeah."

"I guess we need to talk with her again," Molly said.

"We do," Jesse said.

Molly smiled, looking at the letter.

"And the dance continues," she said.

# 64

Jesse and Molly met the Free Swingers in the spacious atrium of a big gray shingled house that faced the ocean on Paradise Neck. Jesse was the only man in the room. No husbands attended. Hannah Wechsler was there. Kimberly Clark was not. Jesse stood in the center of the long room, with a view of the ocean at his back. Molly sat on a slipper rocker near him. Everyone else gathered in an extended semicircle facing him.

"Thank you for coming," Jesse said. "Thanks to Mrs. Stevens for allowing us the use of her house."

No one said anything.

"I am not interested as a police chief or a man in the noncriminal private behavior of consenting adults," Jesse said. "But I am looking for a criminal, and you are in a unique position to help me."

They all sat silently. Neatly dressed. A lot of flowered prints. He could have been addressing a group of den mothers, Jesse thought.

"I know you've heard of the Night Hawk. His behavior is essentially voyeuristic. Look but don't touch, so to speak."

"What about that school principal?" a woman asked.

Her voice was hoarse. She cleared it after she spoke.

"We think that may be a different person," Jesse said.

"A copycat?" the woman said.

"Maybe," Jesse said. "But it occurred to me that the Night Hawk might be attracted to a group such as yours. So it would help if you could tell me if there's anyone you've encountered in the activities of your group that looks but doesn't touch."

Everyone looked at Jesse without speaking. Jesse waited.

"That's not allowed," a woman said finally.

"Would you know?" Jesse said. "Would you always know who was doing what with whom?"

Again there was silence. Then several of the women began to shake their heads.

"You wouldn't," Jesse said.

The woman who had cleared her throat cleared it again and then said, "No."

"Okay," Jesse said. "Officer Crane is going to hand out some index cards and pencils. I'd like each of you to list the name of any man with whom you've had experience who has watched and nothing else."

"You think this guy is in our group?" one of the women asked.

"Yes," Jesse said.

"Who do you think he is?"

"Can't say."

"Why do you think so," the woman said. "Because we are a little unconventional, maybe?"

She was a big dark-haired woman with a long braid in her hair.

"We have some evidence," Jesse said.

"What do you think of what we do," the woman with the braid said to Jesse.

"I think it's legal," Jesse said.

"Would you do it?" the woman said.

Jesse was quiet, thinking about it.

"No," he said after a moment. "Probably not."

"What a waste," the woman with the hoarse voice said.

All the women laughed, including Molly.

"Do we have to sign the card?" a woman asked.

"No," Jesse said. "And if there is no one in your experience, just don't write on the card."

Molly handed out cards and pencils.

A woman wearing large tinted glasses raised her hand.

"I have a question," she said.

Jesse nodded at her.

"Can we keep the pencil afterward?" she said.

The women giggled. Jesse laughed.

"Sure," he said. "Swap them around if you'd like."

The women giggled again, and most of them wrote on their cards.

"If there's anyone who took pictures," Jesse said, "without, ah, engaging, I'd like to know that man's name, too."

"No picture taking," the woman with the pigtail said.

"Covert is always possible," Jesse said.

Several women shrugged. No one looked convinced. When they were through writing, Molly walked along the semicircle, picking up the cards. She gave them to Jesse, who slipped them into the side pocket of his coat.

"Anyone have anything else?" he said.

From her seat at the far end of the semicircle, Hannah Wechsler said, "I think this is a witch hunt."

Several of the women looked at her, but none of them spoke. Jesse nodded.

"Anybody else?" he said.

"Are you and Officer Crane going to attend our next meeting?" the woman with the big glasses said.

"Only if somebody calls the cops," Jesse said.

"We'll keep that in mind," the woman said.

# 65

Hannah Wechsler walked into Jesse's office and sat down in a chair. Molly appeared behind her in the doorway and raised her eyebrows. Jesse shook his head faintly.

"You bastard," she said. "You think my husband is the Night Hawk."

"I do," Jesse said.

"I knew you'd find a way to use the Free Swingers against us," she said. "A cop is a cop is a cop."

Jesse said, "I need to ask you an impertinent question."

"You are nothing," she said, "if not impertinent."

"It's a question that needs an answer," Jesse said. "How long has it been since you had sex with your husband."

"Jesus, you are out of control," she said.

"How long?" Jesse said.

"None of your goddamned business," she said.

"Actually, it is," Jesse said.

He took the Night Hawk's last letter from his drawer and gave it to her.

"What's this?" she said.

"Read," Jesse said.

Hannah read the letter carefully, as if Jesse might be trying to trick her. As she finished, her face began to redden. But she clamped her jaw and read it again carefully. When she was done she placed the letter on Jesse's desk, and sat back. The letter lay on the desk at an angle. She leaned forward and carefully squared it to the edge of the desk. She stared at Jesse.

"I got seven names from the swinger women yesterday, of men that watched but didn't touch," Jesse said.

Hannah continued to stare at him.

"All seven names were Seth Ralston," Jesse said.

She continued to stare. Her mouth was a thin, straight line on her red face.

"I had Molly call every woman that was at the meeting, except you," Jesse said, "and ask each of them if Seth Ralston had ever touched them. All of them said no."

Her shoulders hunched and her neck seemed to get thinner.

"You have sex with your husband," Jesse said, "in the last three years?"

Hannah suddenly made a low, harsh screaming sound and doubled over in her chair, hugging her knees and rocking back and forth. As she rocked, the scream changed to a steady keening sound. Molly appeared in the doorway. Jesse put up his hand and nodded that she should stay there. The keening and rocking continued. Molly came in and sat down in the chair next to Hannah and put her arm around Hannah's shoulders. Hannah turned awkwardly toward her and pressed her face against Molly's shoulder. Molly patted her hair. Hannah moaned. Jesse sat silently behind his desk with his arms folded. It took a while, but eventually she got herself under control and sat up. Jesse pushed a box of Kleenex across the desk. She took one and blew her nose, and another and wiped her eyes. Jesse held out the wastebasket, and she discarded the used Kleenex. She took a fresh one from the box and held it, apparently in reserve. She breathed as if she'd been running a long way.

Finally, she said, "I'm sorry."

"I am, too," Jesse said. "Have you not had sex with your husband for three years?"

"At least," she said. "And before that, it was no good."

She looked at Molly.

"I had to work so hard just to . . . get him ready."

Molly nodded.

"All he wanted to do was look and take pictures," she said. "I'll bet there's five hundred nude pictures of me in his computer."

Jesse nodded.

"That's why we joined swingers. I'd get sex out of it. I didn't want to cheat on my marriage. But I like sex. I need it. And he got something out of it without cheating on his marriage."

Jesse nodded again.

"And it didn't occur to you that he might be the Night Hawk?" Jesse said.

She shook her head.

"The closest I got," she said, "was to think, *Wow, here's a guy with the same hang-ups Seth has.* But then I'd think, *Good, Seth has the swingers.*"

"Hard, anyway, to think your husband would do such a thing," Molly said.

"But he did," Hannah said. "He did, he did, he did."

"It was you who told him we were going to have a meeting," Jesse said.

"Yes," Hannah said. "He calls me on his cell phone now and then. It's awkward. I'm straining for conversation."

"Did you tell him about having the meeting?"

"Yes."

"Will you tell him about our conversation?" Jesse said.

"No," she said. "The disgusting little pervert. How could he do this to me. I've tried, Jesus, I've tried. I wanted so much for this to work."

"You love him?" Molly said.

"Half his female grad students were in love with him," Hannah said. "Literary, masculine, adventurous. They thought he was Hemingway. And he cultivated it. Safari jackets, aviator glasses. He even used to have a beard."

"And you were the one that got him."

"Lucky me," Hannah said.

"Do me a favor," Jesse said. "Next time he calls, tell him about this conversation. I want him to know that you know, and I know."

"I can't talk to him anymore," she said. "He makes me want to vomit."

"It'll help us finish this," Jesse said. "He hasn't hurt anybody yet, but he might. And he might miscalculate and get caught and somebody's husband will kill him."

"I don't care," she said. "After what he's done to me? Fuck him."

"Care about the women he may traumatize, care about the husband who might kill him and have to live with that for the rest of his life."

She looked at Jesse for a while as if he puzzled her.

Then she said, "I hadn't thought of it from that angle."

"Tell him enough so he knows we know," Jesse said.

Hannah nodded.

"How the hell am I going to write my dissertation?" she said.

# 66

"My mom said I should write you some kind of thank-you note," Missy Clark said when she came into Jesse's office. "But I said to myself, *No, that sucks. I don't even know what to say.* So I came to see you."

"Good," Jesse said, and gestured at a chair.

"I was right about you," she said. "You're nice."

"I am," Jesse said.

"When I saw you at the school, I thought, *He's a nice man.*"

Jesse smiled.

"And you were right," Jesse said.

"Well," Missy said. "And don't you know it."

"I do," Jesse said.

"My mom and dad are getting a divorce," Missy said.

Jesse nodded.

"No more wife-swapping, "Missy said. "My mom promised."

"How's your brother?" Jesse said.

"He's all screwed up, but my mom says he'll get over it."

Jesse nodded.

"And you?" he said.

"I'm okay," Missy said. "As long as my dad stays the hell away from us."

"He will," Jesse said.

"What if he doesn't?"

"Come and tell me," Jesse said.

"Yes," she said.

"Because?" Jesse said.

"You are the chief of police," Missy said.

"Exactly," Jesse said.

"I heard Mrs. Ingersoll isn't going to be principal anymore," Missy said.

"I think she's taken a leave of absence," Jesse said.

"And I heard she was getting divorced," Missy said.

"I heard that, too," Jesse said.

"Did somebody really take her picture with her clothes off?"

"Yes," Jesse said.

"Was it the Night Hawk?"

"Confidential police information," Jesse said.

"Oh, shit," she said.

"Who am I?" Jesse said.

"I know," Missy said. "I know, the chief of police."

Jesse inclined his head.

"But I like you anyway," Missy said.

"Thank you."

"Why would anybody want a picture of Old Lady Ingersoll undressed?" Missy said.

"Different people need different things," Jesse said.

"I bet she looks icky," Missy said, "anyway."

Jesse made no comment.

"Would you want to see her undressed?" Missy said.

"I don't think she's unattractive," Jesse said.

"But would you want to see her?"

Jesse smiled.

"I just serve and protect," Jesse said. "I don't have likes or dislikes."

"You like my dad?" Missy said.

Jesse smiled again.

"No," he said.

"See," she said.

"You like him?" Jesse said.

"I don't think so," she said. "I guess I should, you know, he's my dad. You're supposed to love your dad."

"There's no right or wrong to it," Jesse said. "You have no control over who he is. But you have the right to control how you feel about him."

She nodded.

"If I don't love him, I don't love him," Missy said.

"It might be more complicated than that," Jesse said. "But for now, it is what it is, and it's not your fault."

She nodded. They both sat for a moment without speaking.

Then Missy said, "Well, I just wanted to thank you."

"You're welcome," he said.

She stood and went to the door and stopped and looked at him. Jesse waited.

"I'm a little scared," she said. "I mean,

my dad's gone. My mom says she's gonna be different. My little brother is weird. I don't know what's going to happen."

"I'm here," Jesse said. "Come see me anytime."

She nodded and looked as if she wanted to say more. But she didn't. She just smiled at him and left.

# 67

Jesse, you nosy bastard!

Proud of yourself? Because you think you know who I am? Nobody really knows who I am. Maybe not even I know who I am. Am I me? Or am I Mr. O? Or am I two people at the same time? Can you figure that one out, Jesse? You may have to. You had no business telling my wife about me. She told me you showed her my letter. She said she never wanted to speak with me again. I guess it can get lonely at the top, huh, Jesse? Or the people in the swingers' group. They'll gossip among themselves. They'll compare notes. They'll figure out who I am, and then it will be all over town. And my life is ruined. I'll get fired from my job. I won't be able to get another one anywhere. Academia is a closed club. The Mr. O rap will follow me everywhere I go. What I have to do, I know, is leave town and take Mr. O with me, and start over. I'll change my name. Maybe I'll be a professional hunter, or take people into the Grand Canyon on muleback. You know who I am, but you can't find me and I'm about to disappear. Better move fast. I'll give you a little help. Before I go I'm going to uncover one more secret, photograph it, and send you a copy. My farewell card, so to speak. You might be surprised when you find out who it is. Here's a hint. She's someone you're close to!!! So stay alert, my friend. It's your last chance. . . . And like they used to say in the movies, I WON'T BE TAKEN ALIVE!

                      **The Night Hawk**

# 68

Jesse sat in his office with Molly and Suit. The door was closed.

"We got anything on where Seth Ralston is?" Jesse said.

"Haven't found him. Haven't located his car. Moll says he used an ATM in the Bay State Mall to withdraw five hundred dollars, and another one in a hotel lobby in Cambridge, to take out another five hundred dollars."

"That's it?"

"That's it," Suit said.

"A mall on the highway, and a hotel lobby in Cambridge," Jesse said.

"That tell you anything?" Suit said.

"Only that he's got a car."

"Which we already knew," Suit said.

"You got his plate numbers on the wire," Jesse said.

"You bet," Suit said.

"Moll?" Jesse said. "Anything to add?"

"Nope. No credit-card activity. No bank activity except the two ATMs. No other withdrawals, no checks written," Molly said.

"I thought he'd be easier to find," Jesse said.

"He seems to have given it some thought," Molly said.

"Smart guy," Suit said.

"For a professor," Jesse said.

He handed out photocopies of the last letter from the Night Hawk.

"God," Suit said. "The poor sonovabitch is crazy, isn't he."

"You figured out who this person close to you is?" Molly said. "Does he know about Jenn?"

"I don't know how he would," Jesse said. "And even if he did, how would he know where she is. Hell, I don't know where she is."

"You been seeing Sunny Randall again," Suit said.

"Couple of times," Jesse said, "at the Gray Gull. He'd have to have seen us there, ID'ed her, find out where she lives. Seems like a long shot to me."

"Yes," Molly said. "To me, too."

"How about Mrs. Ingersoll?" Suit said. "He's probably mad at her, anyway, for saying he did something he didn't do."

"Possible," Jesse said.

"Marcy Campbell is an even longer shot than Sunny Randall," Molly said.

"Yes," Jesse said.

"You have a thought?" Molly said.

"I have a theory," Jesse said. "If you were Seth the Night Hawk, and you didn't know anything much about me except that I was chief of police, and you began to sort of watch me, ask around about me, that sort of thing. What woman would be most frequently and closely associated with me?"

"It can't be Rita Fiore," Suit said.

Jesse shook his head.

He sat quietly while Molly and Suit thought about it. They didn't think of anyone.

"It doesn't necessarily have to be a romantic relationship," Jesse said. "What woman do I simply spend the most time with?"

"Me," Molly said.

Suit turned to look at her, then back at Jesse.

"Molly?"

"That would be my theory," Jesse said.

"I think so," Molly said.

Unconsciously, Suit's hand rested lightly on his gun butt.

"You think he would actually take a run at Molly?" Suit said.

"She's often with me. She's a woman. She has a secret."

"And a damn good-looking one," Molly said.

Suit flinched.

"Jesus, Moll," he said.

She smiled at him.

"We won't let it happen," Jesse said, more for Suit than for Molly.

"I'll stay with her," Suit said. "Anytime she's not in the office with you, I'll be right there."

Molly was shaking her head.

"I appreciate your concern, but you guys aren't thinking about it right," she said.

"What's the right way?" Jesse said.

"We want this to happen, it's our shot at this creep, maybe, if we believe him, our last one."

"You want to be bait," Jesse said.

"No," Suit said.

"Yes," Molly said. "I'm a cop. I'm not the girl who makes coffee and pats down the female perps. I'm a cop. I have a gun, and Mace. I know something about self-defense. And I'm pretty sure I'd have backup."

"Molly," Suit said. "For crissakes . . ."

Jesse put his hand up to stop Suit.

"She's right," Jesse said.

Molly looked at him.

"You came around pretty easy," she said.

"When you're right, you're right," Jesse said.

"You devious sonovabitch," Molly said. "You knew I'd say that, didn't you?"

"I like a volunteer," Jesse said.

## 69

"My husband is fishing with his brother," Molly said.

They had moved to the squad room so Jesse could walk back and forth as they talked and write things on the chalkboard.

"Where?" Jesse said.

"Trawler's going up off George's Bank," she said.

"How long are they usually out?"

"Till the boat's full," Molly said. "Couple weeks, anyway."

"He's not carpentering anymore?" Suit said.

"Does that, too, "Molly said. "Does a lot of things. Mostly what he wants to."

"Like what?" Suit said.

"Carpenters, works in the boatyard, fishes with his brother, does some lobstering, crews now and then on one of the yachts."

"Sounds like a pretty good life," Suit said. He looked sideways at Jesse and grinned. "No boss."

"Michael couldn't work a regular job," Molly said. "He'd eventually get fired, or punch out the boss."

"And then get fired," Suit said.

Molly shrugged.

"I'm the one with the steady job," she said.

"You talk to Mike while he's gone?" Jesse said.

"Cell phone," Molly said. "We usually talk every day."

"You going to tell him about this?"

"I don't know," Molly said. "He deserves to know, but he'll worry, and he's a hundred miles at sea."

Jesse nodded.

"You'll decide," he said.

"Yes," Molly said.

"If you do decide to tell him, be sure he keeps it to himself. He's probably not the only guy with a cell phone."

"And word gets around," Molly said. "I know."

"How 'bout the kids?" he said.

"Get the bus at the end of the street at ten past eight," Molly said. "Come home at three-thirty, except for my oldest, who usually doesn't get home until supper."

"What are we going to do about them?" Jesse said.

"They'll have to be covered," Molly said. "That's my only rule in this."

Jesse was looking out the squad-room window.

"Can they go visit somebody for a while?" he said.

"For a day or two, sure," Molly said. "My sister lives in Newburyport and they get along with their cousins."

"This may be more than a day or two," Jesse said.

He turned from the window and walked the length of the room and leaned a shoulder against the wall next to the door.

"I know," Molly said. "And they can't miss

that much school, and, frankly, I won't send them away for that long. I miss them."

Jesse nodded. He walked back to the window. He looked out.

"Okay," he said. "Either of you got a contact at the town paper?"

Suit smiled.

"Used to date the editor," he said.

"And she's forgiven you?" Jesse said.

"She's grateful as hell," Suit said.

"Good," Jesse said. "We want to plant a story."

"What story?" Suit said.

Jesse turned and walked halfway down the room and leaned on the conference table, his palms flat on the tabletop.

"We'll work that out in a minute," Jesse said. "Moll, tell me about your neighborhood."

# 70

It was a shabby room in a shabby motel on the highway, where most people stayed only a few hours. But it had a bathroom and a bed, and the sheets seemed clean. The Night Hawk sat on the edge of the bed with his laptop, reading *The Paradise Town Crier* online.

### Paradise Mom Balances Family and Police

Michael Crane recently shipped out for George's Bank on his brother Bob's trawler, *Sea Crane*. Mike leaves behind his wife, Molly, who is a full-time mother, wife, and police officer. And with her husband absent periodically for weeks at a time, Molly must juggle things even more adroitly. "Chief Stone has been great," Molly says. "He gives me the freedom to do what I need to do as a mother. He has arranged my schedule so that I am home every morning to get the kids off to school and do the housework." Molly Crane grew up in Paradise, as Molly Mulherne. She met her future husband in the fourth grade, and, she says, they have been together ever since. . . .

There was a picture of Molly Crane that looked as if it was taken from her high school yearbook. She didn't look that different, he thought, but different enough for his purposes. He'd studied her long enough and closely enough to see it. The story went on, and he read it to the end. The writing was amateurish, of course, like the writing in all those small-town local papers. And the information was good. He had at least a two-week window to make his final discovery in Paradise. For a moment he considered whether this was a plant, and Jesse was trying to trap him. *No,* he decided. *Old Jess isn't that smart. Time,* he thought, *to hop on the bus, and reconnoiter.*

# 71

"Everybody's got a picture of Seth Ralston," Jesse said to Suit.

"They have. I got his license picture from the registry and personally gave each guy a blowup," Suit said.

"Okay," Jesse said. "Moll?"

"Paradise police cruiser parked on the street outside Betsy Ingersoll's house," Molly said. "Twenty-four-seven."

"Who?" Jesse said.

"Buddy, Paul, and Steve," Molly said. "Eight hours each. Four on, four off."

"They know it's a head fake?" Jesse said.

"No," Molly said. "I hoped it would help them pay attention if I told them we had reason to think the Night Hawk might make his move on her."

"Agree," Jesse said.

"I talked to the Dorseys," Jesse said. "They said we can sit in their upstairs guest bedroom and watch your house."

"Why them?" Molly said. "I'm a lot closer to the Hanleys."

"No kids," Jesse said. "I don't want everybody in the Paradise public school system to be talking about this."

"Good point," Molly said. "I've not told my kids anything about it. Tell Arthur to be in civilian clothes riding the bus, or they'll wonder. If he's just another adult, they won't even notice him."

"How 'bout your husband?" Jesse said.

"I told him. He'll keep it to himself."

"How'd he handle it," Jesse said.

"It's probably good he's not here," Molly said. "I think he'd hide in the bushes and jump the first guy that approached the house."

"Don't blame him," Jesse said. "You fight?"

"No," Molly said. "Now and then I'm

reminded of what kind of man he is. He said he knew I was a cop when he married me. He knew I could take care of myself. And he knew we couldn't have the marriage we have unless I was free to do what I needed to do."

"He said that?" Suit said.

Molly nodded.

"He understood why you had to do this?" Suit said

"There's a reason I married him, you know," Molly said.

"I've talked to Peter Perkins," Jesse said. "He doesn't know quite what's up, but he's prepared to run the shop while you and me and Suit are on, ah, special assignment."

"That's it?" Molly said.

"Yep, even in the department, I don't want more people to know than have to."

"You and Suit and me," Molly said.

"You'll wear a gun, all the time, like we agreed."

"Under my clothes," Molly said. "So if it gets to that, I can get it as I disrobe."

"Where you gonna wear it?" Suit said.

"None of your business," Molly said.

"And the wire?" Jesse said.

"Mike in my bra, transmitter pack in the

small of my back. He won't see it unless you're late getting there."

"You'll turn it on the minute he shows," Jesse said.

"I will."

"We need to time this right," Jesse said. "I want him to make his move, so there's no doubt that we got him."

"Hey, Moll," Suit said. "What if we're a little late getting there and when we bust in to rescue you, you're standing around in your underwear?"

"I thought of that," Molly said. "So I've ordered up some new cute undies and charged it to the department."

Jesse smiled.

"We won't be late," he said.

"We won't?" Suit said. "Damn!"

# 72

It was a nice morning. The Night Hawk carefully screwed the stolen license plates onto his Crossfire. He had already put his plates on the little red Audi convertible that he'd stolen these plates from. If he was lucky, especially if it was a woman's car, she wouldn't even notice that her plates were wrong. The Audi looked like a chick car. There was a big smiley face hanging from the rearview mirror. When he finished putting on his new plates, he got in the car and looked at himself in the rearview mirror. He had a heavy beard. And he hadn't shaved since he went underground. His beard was already sufficiently thick. He liked the beard, even the gray streaks. Distinguished. He put on some sunglasses. He felt the small weight of his derringer in the pocket of his black windbreaker. He liked the derringer. He'd never actually fired it, but he had dry-fired it enough. And it was romantic. It was the right gun for the Night Hawk.

He put the car in gear and prowled out from behind his scruffy building and onto the highway. Time to reconnoiter. He drove carefully, keeping inside the speed limit, cruising easily in the right lane. He turned off into Paradise and passed within a block of his condo. That was over. He'd miss Hannah, maybe, a little. But he knew her secret far too well. He smiled to himself. And she knew his. It had probably been a mistake to marry her. But he'd believed the pretense. He'd thought her open and nonjudgmental surface was real. He'd thought maybe she could help him. But she hadn't. She hadn't helped him with any of it. He was probably not the marrying kind. It was a mistake he wouldn't make again. He never thought ahead very far; mostly it was from one escapade to the next. Discovery to discovery. But now, for the first time in a while, he was ending something and moving on. To what? Jesse knew who he was. So did Hannah. Soon it would be common knowledge. He'd have to go a far distance and start over. He wouldn't probably have much luck getting an academic job. Hard to get references. He had some cash. He'd been putting cash aside for years, in case. He didn't know where yet. Anonymous city, small room, practice his craft of discovery. Maybe a little less effete in his next life. Maybe escalate a little. Stay unencumbered. Stay solitary.

He drove along the western shoreline toward downtown. He passed the Ingersoll house. A Paradise police cruiser was parked outside. He smiled. *You think I'm after her, Jesse. Not a bad guess. I would like to see that picture. But I'm not that stupid.* He drove on into the old part of town. It was a nice town. It was the best place he'd lived since Mr. O had overtaken him. And soon he'd leave it forever. And go somewhere else. And do what he did. For the rest of his life. He turned up Molly Crane's street. Nothing unusual. He drove past her house. Nice. Weathered shingles. Blue shutters. A basketball hoop on the garage. Domestic. *Well, we'll shake that up a little, won't we?* He turned in the cul-de-sac at the end of the street and drove back down. He went up the next street, where he could look through and see her backyard. Everything as it should be. He circled the neighborhood a few times. No cops. No cruisers. Nothing unusual. He looked at the dashboard clock. Ten-thirty. *Why not? Why not now?* He felt his chest tighten. He felt the feeling in his belly. He turned back around the block and onto her street. She'd have taken her shower by now. And dressed in clean clothes. Probably making beds now, and doing laundry and cleaning house. He parked at the corner of the street and got out. He didn't need the ski mask this time. They knew who he was already. He began to walk up the street toward her house with the derringer in the right-hand pocket of his jacket, and his camera in the left. She was a policewoman. *What if she had a gun? Probably not doing housework. But what if she could get it?* Well, he had a gun. He felt the small jag of fear push past the other feelings.

That was both good news and bad. It was the police part that was so enticing. The badge and gun were no match for the Night Hawk. The uniform stripped away. The secret revealed. He'd have his pictures. And he'd be gone. And next week he'd have new territory to explore. New secrets to reveal. In the next town. And the next. For the rest of his life. *God!* His heart was beating hard now, and his breathing was quick. He was afraid. But the desire smothered the fear. He had jumped off the cliff. There was no stopping himself now. He reached her front door. He turned the knob and it opened. Very quietly, he went in.

# 73

In the kitchen, Molly hung up the phone and turned on the wire. When she went into the living room she had to fake the surprise, because Jesse had just told her he was coming in. But she didn't have to fake the fear. That was real. He pointed the little silver derringer at her.

"Who are you?" she said.

"I think you know," he said.

"What do you want?" she said.

"I think you know that, too," he said.

"You're the Night Hawk," she said.

"Yes."

"What do you want?"

"Remove your clothes," he said.

His voice sounded to Molly as if it had a small quiver in it.

"Remove my clothes?"

"Now," he said.

"In front of you?"

"I like to watch," he said.

"And if I refuse?"

"I'll shoot you," he said.

"Don't do that," Molly said.

"Then start the striptease," he said.

"Yes, sir," Molly said. "Here I go."

She began slowly to unbutton her shirt. *Come on, Jesse,* she thought. *If Suit actually sees me in my underwear, I'll shoot myself . . . or him.*

"What's so funny," the Night Hawk said.

"There's nothing funny," Molly said.

"You were smiling."

Molly unbuttoned the last button on her shirt.

"I do that when I'm nervous," Molly said.

"Take off the shirt," he said.

*Shirt isn't bad,* she thought. *Line of duty and all that.* But she had taped a gun to the inside of her right thigh. If she dropped her skirt, he'd see it, and then what? If she had to drop the skirt, she'd come up with the gun. And the hell with Jesse and Suit.

She didn't have to. Looking past Seth Ralston, she saw the knob turn silently on her front door. She began to beg loudly.

"Please," she said. "Please don't make me do this. Please."

It covered any sound of entry, and, she could see, it pleased Ralston.

"Sorry, honey," Ralston said. "The clothes gotta come off. The quicker they do, the quicker it's over."

"Freeze right there," Jesse said.

Ralston turned his head and saw Jesse, and Suitcase Simpson, each with a gun drawn and aimed, Jesse to his right rear, Suit to his left. He looked back at Molly. She had her gun out from under her skirt.

"It's a trap," he said.

"Yes, it is," Molly said. "Put the gun down."

Ralston looked back at Jesse. There was a little earpiece in Jesse's left ear.

"You figured this out," Ralston said.

"Put the gun on the ground," Jesse said.

Ralston stared at Jesse and glanced at

Suit and looked back at Molly. Nobody moved. Ralston lowered the gun.

"The end of the Night Hawk," he said.

"Put the gun on the floor," Jesse said.

"Jail time."

"Put it down now," Jesse said. "I won't tell you again."

"We know naught of our coming hither or our going hence," he said. "Readiness is all."

He raised the derringer suddenly and leveled it at Molly, and all three cops fired. Ralston went down in a heap and lay still on the floor. The three cops looked down at him. Jesse crouched and felt for a pulse and found none and stood.

"Dead," Jesse said.

Silently, Suit holstered his weapon and picked up Molly's shirt from where she had dropped it on the floor. He draped it over her shoulders.

"I wonder which one of us killed him," Molly said.

"All of us," Jesse said.

"At his request, I think," Molly said.

# 74

Jesse sat in the warm evening with Sunny Randall on his small balcony. She had a martini. He had a scotch. It was a clear night. There were stars. And in the bright moonlight they could see the outline of Paradise Neck, with its lighted windows looking a bit starlike as well.

"All three shots were fatal?" Sunny said.

"According to the ME," Jesse said.

"Shooting team give you an okay?" Sunny said.

"Yep. Healy led the team. Necessary lethal force."

"Good," Sunny said. "How do you feel about it?"

"Had to be done," Jesse said.

"I know," Sunny said. "But how do you feel about it?"

Jesse sipped his scotch. He smiled at Sunny.

"Had to be done," he said.

"Oh," Sunny said. "I see."

Jesse looked at her for a while.

"You've done it," Jesse said. "How did it make you feel?"

"Had to be done," Sunny said.

"Exactly," Jesse said.

"And the others?" Sunny said.

"Molly's fine," Jesse said. "I think she thought he deserved to be shot. Suit? I don't know. It's hard to figure sometimes what Suit is thinking."

"Probably makes it easier that you all killed him," Sunny said.

"Like a firing squad," Jesse said.

They sat quietly. No boats moved in the harbor. The gulls were quiet. There was no breeze, just the faintly cool ocean scent that drifted up to them. Jesse got up and made them each another drink.

As he finished, the phone rang. He looked at the caller ID.

"I have to take this," Jesse said. "It won't be long."

"I'll close the French doors," Sunny said.

"No," Jesse said. "It's Jenn. I want you to listen."

Sunny looked at him but said nothing. Jesse picked up the phone.

"Jesse," Jenn said. "Oh, thank God you're there."

"I'm here," Jesse said.

"Things are terrible," Jenn said. "I don't know what to do. I've been fired. They are restructuring the whole show. I don't know what to do."

"How about your producer friend," Jesse said.

"He's the one that fired me," Jenn said.

"No business like show business," Jesse said.

"What am I going to do?" Jenn said.

"Another job?" Jesse said. "Another producer? Whichever comes first."

"Don't tease me, Jesse. I'm frantic. I need you. I need to come there and be with you."

"No," Jesse said.

"No?"

"No."

"Jesse, please," Jenn said. "I need this."

"No," Jesse said. "No more."

"No more?"

"It's done, Jenn," Jesse said. "We're done. I won't do this anymore."

"Jesse, do you hate me so much?"

"I don't hate you, Jenn. I just want you out of my life."

"Jesse," Jenn said, "Jesse. I can't. I don't . . . I don't know what to do."

"Your problem, Jenn."

"Jesse, please, what happened to make you turn on me like this?"

Jesse took in some air. There was a long, complicated answer to that question, and Jesse thought he knew what it was. He looked at Sunny. Sunny was motionless, watching him.

"Stuff happens," he said, and gently hung up the phone.

He picked up the drinks and walked to the balcony and handed Sunny hers. She took it and smiled at him.

"You understand what went on there?" Jesse said.

"I believe so," Sunny said.

"What do you think?"

"I think it bodes well," Sunny said.

She put one hand up, and gently Jesse high-fived her.